THE WOOD AND THE TREES

Also by Mary Elgin

A MAN FROM THE MIST

HIGHLAND MASQUERADE

THE WOOD
and
THE TREES

by
MARY ELGIN

M. S. MILL CO., INC. *distributed by*
William Morrow & Company, Inc.
New York 1967

Second Printing, March 1967

Printed in the United States of America.

CONTENTS

Nel mezzo del cammin di nostra vita
mi ritrovai per una selva oscura,
chè la diritta via era smarrita.

Dante: La Divina Comedia

Part One

CHAPTER 1

Wednesday, Thursday, Friday, and then it happened. I was released from rhythmic drabness, only to plunge into ice-cold uncertainty.

The take-over had long been worrying us. We were an old-established firm of excellent reputation but there were soon indications that the new masters were impatient with our quiet tempo. These brooms intended to sweep prodigiously clean.

Twenty-four of us! It was smoothly done. A more than adequate check in lieu of formal notice, a grudging reference, and we scattered, avoiding each other's eyes, our debts and burdens etched across our faces. I had been a minor executive for some ten years, with more experience than qualifications, but now diplomas outweighed acquired wisdom. The future was murky.

"It's worse as you get older," I heard someone say. Was it? I could remember the last time, when I was a young, unemployed widow with little ones clinging to my skirts, and insecurity like a chasm in front of me. Anything was better than that.

An ill wind hit me as I left the building, tugging at my shabby coat, now well into its third season. So that was the end of Marietta Brandon, Personnel Officer, a middle-aged woman walking more slowly than usual. Strange I should have been reasonably successful at managing others, when I had no skill with my family or myself!

For the first time in years, I did not turn automatically toward the tube-station. I had entered limbo, deprived of the right even to play the automaton. Unfamiliar thoughts and reactions shuffled in my head and demanded my whole attention. Predominant was an unexpected and quite impractical relief.

Change had been forced upon me, and at that moment had a positive, soothing quality. There was a limit to the number of times you could retrace the pattern of weeks and years. I could have chosen more adventurous ways of earning a living, after all, but a decade of conservatism had narrowed the choice and the chooser. Bills, one had come to believe, were paid in a currency of boredom.

I walked on absentmindedly and was surprised to find myself in the park under the trees. The sky was dark with the ocher heaviness of London and a cold rain was spitting on the grey grass. A female Dante, lost in the dark wood, the *selva oscura* of middle age. Divine comedy! Curious sense of humour!

I sat on a damp bench and shivered. It was not a wise thing to do. After struggling grimly through the prevalent influenza, ignoring doctor's orders in a useless attempt to earn reprieve when the ax fell, I was now vulnerable, abjectly tired, and my aching, addled head incapable of initiative or enterprise. A sad candidate for a place in the concrete jungle.

"I'm forty-one," I told myself. "The prime of life." Absurd statement! My back ached, a harsh cough plagued me, and a nagging pain lurked in my left side. Hope and optimism were throttled by physical discomfort; even regret eluded me. I couldn't long nostalgically to be young again. I remembered youth too clearly.

To shake off my black mood, I told myself again I was better off than a decade before, when the boys, already at their expensive private school, were growing a size a term, and Renata had been ailing, a ghost of a child. That tiny flat must have been unhealthy and its rent was scandalous. Yet in those days, I had been strong and resolute, determined on better things. Time is debilitating.

Geoffrey would soon be twenty-two, Michael would be twenty-one this year, and Renata was already begging to leave school. But was less money really needed? Were they more self-sufficient? My responsibility had diminished very little and I felt it the more onerous for having borne it longer.

The rain fell heavily, dripping monotonously off the plane trees. Only the distant streetlamps relieved the absolute darkness of nightmare.

Selva oscura. The theme returned uneasily. "Another part of the wood. I've been here before, bitter and lonely, the straight path lost." Looming trees hemmed me in; they were huddled too closely together. Inferno, purgatory, yes; but where was paradise?

I couldn't afford self-pity. Take a grip! Geoffrey would be an architect one day, if only he would work harder. Michael would soon finish at Cambridge, and I must dissuade him from further training. There was enough to see Renata through "A" Levels, if she could be made to recognize their importance. The educational struggle didn't last for ever.

One day I should be free, and too tired to care. Years of emancipation, empty and pointless. My own company and Dante's. Lord!

It was lucky I'd been sacked in a crowd. Better than being

singled out for exhausted inefficiency. Sleep, knitting up the ravelled sleeve of care. How does one cure insomnia? I was good at pretense. It had been the hobby of a lifetime. It would all seem better tomorrow. Aspirins clear the head; one parent is as good as two; get up, go home, pull yourself together.

Despite my delay, the train was still crowded with comrades in pallor and discouragement. I was cold and wet. I'd behaved like a silly child. You can't be ill in the holidays. Dispose of children through necessity, and you must make it up to them when you can. There are rules laid down for parents. Once it had been children who followed the blueprint. I seemed to get the rough end of each generation.

I missed my bus at the station and decided to walk. It had stopped raining, but the cold air was still laden with moisture. My feet were dragging, my pain stabbed. As I turned the final corner, I almost collided with Geoffrey running for the bus.

"Oh, there you are! I couldn't wait. I'm meeting Helga." He sounded reproachful.

Michael was holding on for a long-distance telephone call.

"You're late, Mother. Ren's struggling with dinner." He sounded hungry.

Renata was pushing back her pale-gold tent of hair. She was flushed, and there was grease on her new Italian sweater.

"I've put on the meat. What on earth happened to you? The boys are rampaging, unless G. has given you up as a bad job. Why didn't you let us know?"

"Sorry. I'll take over."

"Thank goodness! I want to wash my hair! And by the way . . . before I forget . . . Aunt Anglesey telephoned."

"What had she to say?"

"Wanted to know how you were. Seemed to think you were ill. You aren't, are you?"

The answer was obviously a defiant lie.

"That's what I told her. Oh yes . . . and she asked us all to lunch on Sunday. Twelve sharp. And won't take no for an answer."

"I'd be the last person to refuse," I said very slowly. "I'd better tell you. I've lost my job, Renata."

"Good!" said my daughter in reply.

CHAPTER 2

An invitation from my aunt, Beatrix Anglesey, is our nearest equivalent to a Royal Command. We cancel more casual engagements, get out our best clothes, and make our pilgrimage to Falloden Street, neat as Alice's oysters, and far more apprehensive.

When the children were small, they could imagine what life was like on Mount Olympus, for what goddess was more omnipotent than their Aunt Beatrix? Or could ambrosia compare with her Lucullan spreads? More an agent of fate than its victim, she appeared to grasp destiny like a nettle, immune herself, but dangerous to those nearby. She was our arbiter, and our friend.

In the drawing room at Falloden Street, eighteenth-century elegance imposed order on our habitual chaos. Instinctively my three Brandons had formed a conversation piece which a sleepless night and a mounting temperature allowed me to study with immense detachment. Michael was in his favourite position, central on the hearthrug, dominating the scene. Energy radiated from him till it devitalized the rest of

13

us. He overtopped his elder brother by several inches and made the most of the advantage. He was the family trouble-maker.

Beside him, Geoffrey looked graceful and immature. He had chosen the largest armchair and had spread himself over it like butter. A good-looking boy, if his features had not lacked incisiveness. He moved like a dancer but without a dancer's deliberation; his soft, fair curls were too pretty and young; his sensitive hands were restless. He was intelligent, talented and good-natured, but his lazy dislike of competi-tion, his apologetic choice of the easiest course, alarmed me, when there was nothing more urgent to claim my anxiety.

"Sit up straight," I now ordered automatically. "You're not lounging about at home. And incidentally, I hope you'll all behave yourselves today. We owe Aunt Trix so much, and we may yet have to owe her more."

Another is the nearest thing I know to the proverbial water polishing the adjacent stone.

"Darling, we *know*. You've said it often enough." Renata was poised over an outsize bowl of hyacinths, fresh and ra-diant as spring itself. At seventeen, she was fining down to something very near beauty. Dark, wide-set eyes, almost in-digo in colour, were swept by black lashes which contrasted strangely with her pale moonlight hair. I wondered suddenly what dangers were inherent in such development, and no-ticed for the first time the growing petulance of her mouth.

"I'll say this for our interesting aunt," Michael was saying, "she doesn't ram her charity down the throat. Now Gran or Aunt Peg you have to thank a dozen times, preferably on your knees, for one monogrammed handkerchief. Old Trix doesn't bat an eyelid at a fiver."

"She has more money than your grandmother," I re-proved.

"So it does her no harm to succour the widow and orphan."

"For goodness' sake, Mike! She'll be back any moment." Renata looked genuinely nervous, even as she giggled.

"I agree," Geoffrey contributed. "Helga was saying that as we're the only representatives of the present generation, it's natural she should give mother a helping hand."

Michael drew his black eyebrows together in a characteristic frown.

"Helga," he snapped, "is a complete clot, and I don't see it's any business of hers."

"It could be," Geoffrey drawled.

"Poor old G.! Is she tightening the noose? *'We're only young once, Geoffrey!'* " Mike could mimic with quite appalling accuracy.

"Oh shut up!" his brother said. "And mind your own business! I didn't say I was contemplating holy matrimony."

"Can't you two stop quarrelling for five minutes?" Renata intervened. "Fighting's wrong for this room. Wouldn't it be heavenly to live in a house like this all the time; have maids, flowers, and buy everything you want with piles and piles of money?"

"Typical," Michael retorted. "You've the mentality, Ren, of a Persian cat. Bet you'd soon run through every penny."

"Personally, I'd rather have a Bentley," Geoffrey contributed conversationally. "How about you, Mike?"

He shrugged, but we all knew the answer. Michael had a peculiarly one-track mind which saw no further than a triumphal progress from First-Class Honours to Q.C., if not Attorney-General. It seemed an awkward ambition for a completely indigent young man, till one remembered uneasily that Mike never tolerated half-measures, and was the stubbornest thing in nature.

15

How frustrating, I thought absently, to be born to genteel poverty and bred to ape the rich without any of their resources. Better perhaps to have given my children the laissez-faire freedom of working-class life, but like a buoyant log, I could not sink. Thus, while they continued to talk in thousands, I glumly totted up my pence. When I had covered the outstanding bills, the holiday I needed so badly would be as far away as ever.

"At least I don't throw away money on girls," Michael was saying virtuously.

"Don't get the chance," Geoffrey grinned. "The girl who cleaved or clove to you, dear brother, would of necessity be a tragic heroine or a complete maniac—probably the latter."

"Enough of that," I interposed hastily. "Why must you boys always brawl? We so seldom go out as a family nowadays. Let's enjoy ourselves."

"At Sunday lunch with Aunt Trix?" Renata pulled a face. "Why are we here, anyway?"

"The whys and wherefores don't matter," I replied. "I'm glad enough to relax without having to cook and wash up."

"Mother's feeling long-suffering," Michael observed.

"Not without cause," I snapped back at him.

I spoke far more sharply than I had intended and they were disconcerted into silence. A quiet and apparently peaceful scene, therefore, was presented to Beatrix Anglesey on her entry. No one within living memory had kissed her by way of greeting. She despised the usual conventions and preferred to survey her field and open the batting herself.

"A handsome family!" she now remarked. "But let's not forget that dismal proverb. So how do you *do,* dear children —if that's not too indiscreet a question?"

We chorussed demurely while she continued to assess us.

"Sorry I'm late, but Father Mallory grows more and more prolix. Well, Geoffrey! You've lost a beard and gained a haircut since last I saw you—Heaven be praised! As for you, young Michael, I won't inquire. You never improve, you merely grow! And here's my little Ren, pretty as a picture on a chocolate box and about as inspiring. You should tie your hair back, child, or you'll ruin your eyesight."

They smiled dutifully, wary as scholars in the headmaster's study. Aunt Anglesey grimaced and turned her attention to me.

"Poor Mitty!" She raised her startling eyebrows. "I won't waste time in asking how you are. I've never seen anyone look so ill outside a hospital."

I am diffident about describing my father's sister. We had long been conditioned to her and had almost learned to take her for granted. We did not find it remarkable, for instance, that she had elected to attend her High-Anglican church in what appeared to be the riding-habit of young Queen Victoria, nor that her playing card wig supported a headdress rather than a hat. That her extravagance of costume was triumphant rather than ludicrous was due to the personality of the woman herself, which eclipsed all oddities of taste. Deploring the limitations of middle age, it was characteristic of her to circumnavigate them. A car accident in her late thirties gave her the opportunity she needed. An extended convalescence was spent abroad, and she returned with faded youth scrubbed out, a woman already launched into resplendent old age. The effect at first was devastating; *actressy,* my mother used to say scornfully. I myself could remember the day when my aunt would inadvertently sprint for a passing bus, trailing lorgnettes and glory as she ran. But the years passed and gradually she caught up with her own image, her unaltering appearance meanwhile suggesting a stability which was close on immortality.

Her grin had the impish provocation of a younger Winston Churchill.

17

"My affectionate relations! Sherry, now, for everyone, including Ren. I shall drink to your happiness, Geoffrey, for I hear you are contemplating betrothal with that tedious, toothy wench I met in your house. If this should be true, you need all the good wishes you can get."

"We aren't engaged," Geoffrey was stilted. "But Helga is a perfectly nice girl."

"I expect you're prejudiced," she suggested amiably. "Young men often are when flattered. And now, what news of the rest of you?"

"Mother's lost her job," Michael contributed. "She's peeved about it."

"You didn't tell me that, Mitty, though I remember you saying you weren't happy about the way things were going."

"They only pensioned me off on Friday," I replied as lightly as I could.

"And a jolly good thing too," Renata added. "Those new people were slave drivers. It wasn't good enough."

"I wonder if your mother is of the same opinion. An employer is an employer, and pays, whatever the working conditions. And Mitty is surely used to slave driving. At the office, at home; where's the difference?"

"We do our best," my daughter muttered sulkily.

"Evidently not good enough," my aunt said tartly, "You three are a warning against too casual reproduction. Just look at your mother! She's like a wraith. Ah well! Drink up your sherry, Renata, and don't pull faces over it. You can tell your sixth form you're half-way to becoming an incurable alcoholic."

Ordinarily, I would have protested, ranged myself on the side of my children, who, after all, were no worse than any others. Today, however, I found myself hungering for the support of age, detachment and understanding. Aunt

18

Anglesey was another widow, and a far better fighter. Once upon a time, she had looked at me with that infinite humour and barely repressed impatience. The very continuity of the generations steadied me.

"It's a matter of common knowledge," she continued, "that a donkey harnessed to the treadmill goes unthanked by those who most benefit from its industry and stupidity. Poor Mitty is a donkey; but I am a lover of animals."

"Don't pick on me," Renata was getting annoyed. "I've told Mum I'm quite willing to leave school and do my share —but what does she say? Train for this and train for that. I don't want to be ancient before I earn a penny. I live a nunnery life to get 'A' Levels I don't need in subjects which bore me stiff. I'll probably marry before I'm twenty. Mother herself did."

"You flatter yourself," Michael said drily. "Who on earth would marry you, Ren?"

"I must say," even Geoffrey was moved to comment, "you do talk a lot of nonsense, Ren. Marriage is a very serious matter."

"Behave yourselves, children," I interrupted wearily. "You're not at home. What will Aunt Trix think of you?"

"Nothing to their credit," said the lady in question. "And nothing I'm not fully prepared to express. But first we'll lunch and recoup our energies."

As always, I sighed at her dining room. The silver all matched; the china had no blemishes. A huge bowl of jonquils and early tulips was mirrored in a flawless oval table. Aunt Angelesy lived very graciously indeed.

She had the means to do so. The career, like the woman, was interesting. She had refused a millionaire, only to elope with Tom Anglesey, still a mere corporal when he was killed in Flanders. She never looked at another man, though many admired her. The key was turned on that unexpected ro-

19

mance, and she went on alone. It must have been hard for her at first, until Uncle Peregrine, that reputed, or disreputed friend of Oscar Wilde, left her this doll's house in a defiant gesture to a fellow-outcast. She retained the first floor for a luxurious background and in the rest built up her highly successful business, starting with a Domestic Agency but shrewdly riding the tides of social change till she had diversified into several profitable channels. She still supplied servants to the affluent, selecting, of course, the cream of them for herself. She never washed a dish! Impressive thought! Even minor circumstances bent themselves to her will. A clever woman. Meanwhile, her eccentric appearance was a stock-in-trade. Once seen, by employer, by employee, she was never forgotten. As she liked to point out, she was a walking gimmick. Not that money was her chief concern. She found perpetual challenge in the proper ordering of human affairs. Fond as she was of comfort and independence, she remained a woman more interested in others than in herself.

The first course was hardly on the table before she opened fire. I listened half-heartedly, reflecting morosely that she had the same surplus energy as her young victims.

"So you don't hold with higher education, Renata?" she began provocatively. "Is it that you feel you are cut out for an early dedication to the kitchen sink?"

"I don't see the point of more school. As Aunt Peg says, no one wants girls to be too clever, and even if we had the money, it would be silly for me to go to University."

"Interesting you should choose Peggy for your mentor on affairs of the intellect! She derived, I'm afraid, very little benefit from her own education. Fortunately, she was an exceedingly pretty girl, so much was excused her. Is she your pattern?"

20

"Aunt Peg," Renata had strong loyalties, "is a very genuine person."

"Delightful adjective! So apt! Like a dainty, but entirely nonfunctional piece of period furniture, and applies, come to think of it, to your grandmother too. Dear Lucy! So graceful, and so totally useless!"

She went too far. I had to intervene.

"Really, Aunt Trix! Must you demoralize them? They're quite disrespectful enough as it is. As for you, Ren. Why bother to argue? You stay on at school till you have the necessary qualifications to earn your living suitably."

Aunt Anglesey enjoyed such asides, and inspected both of us in turn.

"Yet the child does, albeit accidentally, show a commendable desire to pull her weight in the family. As I see it, she is the only one who does."

"You're a wise woman, Aunt Trix," Michael took his cue smoothly. "Why give the girl Euclid when she wants orange-blossoms, either at the altar or in her much-discussed flower shop? When money's limited, a boy is the better investment, for in the long run he supports the family."

"Whose family?" asked my aunt pointedly.

"I intend to support mother," he explained grandly, "and in more comfort than now. A successful barrister earns a huge income."

"And an unsuccessful one starves."

"I don't intend to be a briefless wonder."

"Brandon, Q.C., the eminent Silk," she grinned. "Self-confidence charms me, but it can be overdone. You choose a singularly inequal profession for your mother to subsidize during your long apprenticeship. In fact, young man, you have ideas above your station."

Michael narrowed his eyes and miraculously kept his temper.

21

"If there's any way of bringing it off, I will," he said. "Money or no money, I've never failed yet. Geoffrey had his precious legacy, but I've earned my education. The trouble is I've demanded too little in the past. I've won exhibitions and scholarships because I've worked for them. I know where I'm going, and what's useful, I can do. I never found a rock face, however tricky, I couldn't climb in the end—with or without ropes."

"Interesting! But how do you achieve your object? Ren, I suppose, leaves school and your future hogs her share. Your mother works, whether she's fit or not. You call up a horrid vision, you know, of your unprotected womenfolk starving, Hogarth-style, while you grow fat eating dinners, or whatever quaint custom entitles you to adjust a barrister's wig to display your admirable profile."

"You don't understand." She was puncturing him at last.

"I understand very well that you're prepared to live on female earnings indefinitely, a young tough like you, happy as a cuckoo in a wren's nest. I hope you don't expect me to reinforce your ambitions."

"There's such a thing as false economy," he argued.

"I cannot imagine," my aunt said, "any of my great-nieces and nephews practicing any economy at all, false or otherwise. And now let's change the subject. Shall it be Brahms, or Benjamin Britten? And have you read any banned books lately?"

Michael glowered at her. He preferred to win his arguments. Geoffrey was already on his second helping, which seemed to require his whole attention. I was feeling sick.

"Uncle Arthur says," Ren stepped into the breach, "that it's all because of *Lady Chatterley's Lover.*"

"What is, child?" My aunt raised her eyebrows.

"Well . . . practically everything."

"The profundity of that remark," Beatrix Anglesey said, "reduces me to silence for the rest of this meal."

22

CHAPTER 3

Back in the drawing room, we were still subdued. The altercation between Michael and his great-aunt affected the rest of us more than the two principals. I wished I felt well enough to smooth out the social creases but the effort was beyond me. Geoffrey and Ren kept out of trouble, and it was Michael, who, after a questioning glance of reproach, coped with the reflux and produced surprisingly pretty party manners, considering how seldom he practiced them.

I surreptitiously slid two codeines into my mouth, and added black coffee to keep me awake. My attention focussed on little, irrelevant things which helped me along from hour to hour. The intermittent nausea which had worried me at table receded to leave an overpowering desire for quiet. If only there were fewer people! If only one of them were not Aunt Anglesey whose eyes were as sharp as her tongue!

It was no consolation to know I was witnessing that increasingly rare phenomenon, my family united against a common enemy. This might be one of the last times they turned to me for support and comfort, and because I was so tired, I should fail them and forfeit my influence, after which my only status would come from a continuing grasp on an empty purse. I accepted a second cup of coffee, then a third, so I could take more interest in what was going on.

"It's remarkable," my aunt was saying, "how young people concentrate upon the future to the exclusion of the present, presumably from sheer laziness. Current problems are so

23

much less maneuvrable for the idle-minded. I often think how obliging destiny was to spare me parenthood. I am far too practical and too impatient. Were I Mitty, or, come to that, a female seagull, I should take an almost fiendish delight in pushing my young over a thousand-foot cliff-drop into the coldest water I could find."

"Whereas I seem to have fallen in it myself." I sounded like a dormouse emerging from a teapot.

"Yes, Mitty," my aunt agreed, "at your age you should be able to fly better. Or do you need a refresher course?"

I drifted away from them again. Birds were very clever and brave to tip their fledgelings helter-skelter down, preening themselves on a deserted ledge, while the little ones dropped like stones toward the jagged rocks below. One summer afternoon, my brother Geoff and I had watched them for hours, our noses buried in hot wild thyme. Herring gulls, marvellously serio-comic, training their brood, long before we ourselves had left the nest.

"Gosh, Mitty! Look at that! Wonderful stall turn! That's what I'd like to do more'n anything else. To fly! And I will."

The children were playing safe by renewing their interminable argument about the relative merits of popular and classical music, Mike and Ren in full opposition, with Geoffrey swinging tolerantly to and fro like a floating voter.

We had seldom grouped into such a threesome in my own family. Nor were we ever an integral party of four. Martin, the eldest, was a star apart. Peg, the baby, had her own exclusiveness. Only Geoff and I in the middle were inextricably linked.

"Wake up, Mitty! Lord! What's amiss with the girl? I've poured you out some tea. Do you know you've slept all afternoon?"

"What's the time?" I asked stupidly, returning from an immense distance. "Where are the children?"

"I softened them up and you did the rest for me. They've never seen you fall asleep like that before and were moderately alarmed, not before time. They went home meekly and Renata has promised to pack you a bag which Geoffrey will deliver this evening. I insist that you stay here with me. No argument."

"I can't possibly! It's exceedingly kind of you, but they mustn't be left high and dry at home."

"Nonsense! Do them good. Nice creatures, but spoiled. You look horribly ill, Mitty. Besides, it would be unfair to your young folk to land them with an invalid during the holidays. Here you can be waited on hand and foot. We'll enjoy it."

"But Mother comes on Wednesday."

"Lucy? Well, that settles everything to perfection. Not only are you in no fit condition to cope with her, but she will give tone to an otherwise unchaperoned establishment. She can, and no doubt will, direct operations."

"Just the same. . . ."

"Mitty, you protest too much! Stop fussing and drink up your tea. If you imagine I'd leave you to the mercies of those young savages in your present state, think again. Besides, it's time they were reformed—and you. I shall announce the finer details of my campaign when I have pondered on them —and you have seen a doctor. You'll not deny, I suppose, that I am capable of running far more complicated households than yours, by remote control, if necessary."

"I suppose I must give in gracefully." I did not add I suddenly enjoyed being bullied. "Just for tonight. I confess, I do feel wretched."

"The doctor will decide the length of your visit, child. I've arranged for dear George to overhaul you in the morning. So relax, Mitty, and be a good girl."

Who hasn't experienced the magic of playing infant in someone else's sphere of authority? I went to bed, grumbling ineffectively, and was forced to drink a nauseating concoction which I suspect contained opium. My aunt had brewed it herself from a Chinese concubine's recipe. It hit me sideways. I slept without a break for twelve hours.

In the morning, I was heavy and listless, though I pretended to feel better. Then the doctor arrived—"dear George"—another of my aunt's creatures, like her bank manager, laywer, priest, and even Pilar, the Spanish girl who played under-nurse. A lot of orders were issued, but my head swam disconcertingly when I made the effort to disobey them. I went back to sleep again as soon as I could.

When next I woke, the curtains were drawn and an open fire burnt brightly in the grate. Aunt Anglesey sat in a large, imported armchair, absorbed in her fine needlework, a Mephistophelean pair of spectacles at the end of her nose. In tranquillity, her surface sharpness faded, to leave a frightening impression of depth and intelligence. She was not really the sort of companion I wanted at that moment.

"Awake at last? Excellent! For it's time you were fed. How shockingly thin you are!"

"I'm all right," I muttered defiantly.

"You're on the brink of pleurisy and pneumonia; you suffer from post-influenzal cardiac strain; you're anemic, partially starved, and a nervous wreck. *Otherwise* you may be *all right,* my child, though, one suspects, rather debilitated. You are ordered to bed for at least a fortnight. No point in risking invalidism at your time of life. Besides, everything goes excellently in your tasteless suburban villa. Lucy is coming a day early. Peg suggested Ren in exchange."

"But I'll be in the clear, if I do stay in bed?" I could control my anxiety no longer. "I won't need a long convalescence? I must get another job soon."

"When I say so, child. Goodness—what's the Government for? All these Benefits—and a generous aunt to boot. I'm told by George you're not to worry. As if, in this frame of mind anyone could stop you! But the financial side, at least, can be shelved."

"And what did you say about straining my heart? I'm not getting into the hands of specialists, am I?"

"I imagine you just need a long rest, and if you behave yourself you'll emerge with a clean bill of health. Specialists? George thinks you should see his tame psychiatrist."

"A psychiatrist? Rubbish!"

"Illness makes you careless. It seems you admitted to George that you are troubled by insomnia, and he thinks this may well account for the deterioration in your physical condition, which obviously started long before your influenza."

"I do sleep badly lately. There's no cure for it. If I dope myself, I have nightmares instead."

"I have always thought insomnia one of the occupational hazards of widowhood. I've often had bouts of it myself." She sounded unconcerned, casually conversational. I fell into the trap.

"I resent it," I said, "because by nature, I'm a very heavy sleeper, and anyhow, I'm generally whacked at the end of my day. Formerly, I merely did some outstanding housework, or read extravagant adventure stories from the boys's bookshelves. It wasn't till I was ill that it got out of hand, and a sort of vicious circle was established. Before, I was exhausted, but not afraid."

"What happened?"

"It's so stupid. One night, I was actually asleep, only I was woken by a horrible pain. I decided there and then, I was

27

going to die and the whole panorama of my life spread out in front of me. I was convinced I had only about five minutes to solve all my problems, repent my sins, and pay my debts to heaven. But the more I considered, the less I understood. It was two o'clock in the morning and, ever since, it's happened regularly, always at the same time, till I lie listening in terror for the grandfather in the hall to strike. It's ridiculous, but I'm scared."

"Why should a retrospect of your life trouble you so?"

"I have to find what went wrong, and when. The difference between faults and misfortunes. To what extent are human beings responsible for their actions? The chessboard is neither white nor black. I'm talking nonsense."

"But *talking*, child. That's important. You've always been a silent person, Mitty. What does it do to you? I've always thought I myself would have made a good psychoanalyst. You'd be surprised how often I act as mother-confessor to total strangers."

"Are you proposing to practice on me?"

"Why not? Wouldn't you prefer me to a gentleman in Wimpole Street? Something must be done about you and it's a solution. I have infinite discretion; I start with a knowledge of the externals. My spare bed is more comfortable than a horsehair couch, and I have always thought moderate doses of Glenlivet in hot milk, the perfect truth drug. Do you think I look like Freud?"

"I think you look like the Prince Regent. Where did you find that dressing gown? I hope you didn't steal it from Brighton pavilion."

"Impertinent chit! Sliding off at a tangent too! I've always been fond of you, child, yet like everyone else, I'm at arm's length. I admit I was never one for confiding my own troubles, and believe that reserve builds up the character in certain cases. But it can, equally, change nature suddenly and become as destructive as a cancer. And that, I'm sure, is what's happening to you. I have at least two weeks to examine the content of your problems."

"And if I don't cooperate?"

Aunt Anglesey lit a cheroot and poured herself a drink.

"So much the better," she replied with an outsize grin.

I stared at her. She was a familiar, comfortable sight. There was a lot in what she said but I had lost the habit of self-revelation. Anyhow, I could offer her only selected, expurgated, botched material. I put the temptation aside.

"You're bracing as ozone, Aunt Trix," I said, "and very, very kind. I'm fond of you too. I don't know if I'd have managed without you." To my annoyance, tears began to roll down my cheeks, and awkwardly I hid them in the pillow. I felt a hand pat me apologetically, as though I were a stray dog, but when I raised my head she was only peering at me, fascinated, through her spectacles.

"I didn't know you could cry," she observed with interest. "And how very tired you must be to let yourself go. I think you should have an eggnog now. Disgusting but strengthening. Your grandmother swore by the mixture. We'll sort you out, never fear."

CHAPTER 4

It was twenty-four hours later and Aunt Anglesey ventured to hope I might yet recover and stopped treating me like thistledown.

"If you have to stay in bed," she observed, "you might as well enjoy it."

When she sat with me in the evening, she was cunning, deciding evidently I was best approached through the children.

"I can't think why you encourage Geoffrey to court this most unsuitable girl. Apart from other material considerations, Geoffrey, more than most, needs a complement. His wife will make or mar him, and this is a self-opinionated hussy—mark my words! And how about Michael? I suppose you know he's being wrongly handled too? Interesting. He's the light of your eyes, but you seldom address a civil word to him. Why does he worry you so?"

"I've often thought women have special talents for special ages. I was better with small children."

"You're a very young mother—that's your trouble."

"On paper. I feel about ninety."

"What I don't see is why you're unfair to Michael. He was quite correct, you know, when he questioned the distribution of wealth. And I know too, that for some reason his education, beyond his own earnings, has always come out of your current wages, or my pocket. You, who are so scrupulous about money."

"Mike was always a favourite sparring-partner of yours," I hedged. "It was easier to ask on his behalf. I've never been in a position to lay aside his scholarship money for him. I could only be grateful that, due to his own efforts, I could educate both boys similarly."

"I wonder why he worked so hard for himself. It was slogging more than natural brilliance."

"He's almost abnormally ambitious."

"And ruthless, self-centered and very able. Another Martin?"

"Martin! Dear God! I hope not."

"I'm not so sure. Why does my query disturb you? Poor Mitty, you look quite wild-eyed. Have a brandy?"

"None of my children . . . ! Michael's *nothing* like Martin. Why should you say so?"

"I suppose not." She ignored my question coolly. "The genes of the Peters aren't very strong. No one like Geoff either."

"Don't you think G. takes after his uncle?"

"Hardly at all. He's far more like John. That disappoints you? At least you're not a hypocrite. It's true I didn't like your husband; nor, I suspect, did you. The boy's better quality, but you must see he marries the right girl. He needs pushing. As for Ren, you're doing no better with her. She's against university or a set profession and you're making her worse. You know she may have the right to her own errors, apart from wasting her time and your income."

"She doesn't know what she wants yet. She's at the silly stage."

"How old were you when you became Mrs. John Brandon?"

"And look what happened to her!" It was out before I realized it.

I don't know why we both laughed, I guiltily, my aunt with a sort of triumph.

"I'll accept that brandy," I said.

It was characteristic of Aunt Anglesey that she did not immediately press her advantage. She took her own dinner in my room, and as far as I remember discussed a book on Egyptian tombs. It was much later when she returned to the attack with new confidence.

"Funny we should talk about John after all these years. I shall always remember the first time I saw you after the funeral. Even your beautiful acting couldn't altogether disguise your relief. The implication was that things had come to such a pass, to be left nearly destitute was an improvement in your lot. In fact, you seemed almost lighthearted."

"I hope no one else thought so! Did you say I wasn't a hypocrite? Ah well! I suppose you're determined to probe, and it was all such a long time ago. John was drunk when he crashed that car, and I was the only who knew it. When the inquest came and went without publicity, the relief was enormous."

"I knew he wasn't temperate latterly."

"He drank like a fish. He was never sober."

"I didn't realize that, Mitty. But of course, you always kept your married life well removed from onlookers."

"Obviously," I retorted bitterly, already regretting this outdated surge of confidence. Point to Aunt Anglesey! I must be more careful. Ridiculous to weaken so long afterwards.

"So now perhaps you can understand why I'd prefer Ren to wait till she has some sense. My own life would have been so different with a more practical start. Why should I, of all people, want my daughter to marry young? Or face the insecure prospect of living by her wits? How much easier it would have been with a profession. Wits are well enough if you keep them alert, but in ill-health or discouragement, they let you down. Look at me now. I can do better for Ren."

My aunt had once again taken up her needlework and was apparently absorbed in interlacing the rich colours of her silks. My own hands were idle, beating a restless tattoo on my immaculate linen sheet.

"Lord! What fools girls are!" I exclaimed. "In love with love and wallowing in my own ignorance. Do you remember The Grange, Aunt Anglesey?"

"I ought to. I was born there."

"A wonderful house! You turned each corner and knew what would come next. It was always poised between spring and high summer with apple trees in blossom beyond the tennis lawn."

"I connect you with that tennis lawn. You were eighteen,

32

I think, when I came to visit, and I remember you were wearing a short, silk tunic. When the set was over, you strolled toward the tea table on the terrace, swinging your racket. You were walnut-brown with charming curls cut very short, like an Athenian youth ripe for suitors."

"What an appalling simile!"

"Reasonably apt. The current image was of a girl with the service of a man. Who could handle a boat, drive a golf ball, or race a car with the best of the males. Who had all the veneer of culture and sport at modest depth. It was your good fortune that you were not only delightful in yourself, but personified the fashionable trend."

"I remember that day too," I ignored her curious tribute. "Everyone was at home: Martin, smoking Russian cigarettes, already down from Oxford. Geoff home on leave, scrambling gratefully into white flannels. Mother, in her forties, I suppose, and extraordinarily attractive. Father and Peg adored her."

"And she, Martin?"

"He was clever—and fascinating. Mother worshipped him. Even Father was glamoured by him. Geoff and I were never able to assess him fairly."

"Is it important? He was mischievous, knowing, and to me, rather slight."

"He was important." I shook my head sadly. "Always. He had power. He worked for it. And he was destructive. He destroyed me."

"Yet you looked very carefree when I saw you," she prompted.

"Why not?" I countered. "It was all ahead of me."

"So you hadn't met John? I remember he wasn't there."

"Wasn't he? But I'd met him years before, and fallen in love. One forgets how early it comes to some people. The sonnets, all a hundred and twenty-five of them, were written

and buried beneath a loose board. I 'found his profile beautiful and rare.' Would you believe it!"

"He was a good-looking boy," my aunt returned equably.
"Geoffrey inherits those small, chiselled features and
cherub's curls. They could both be a girl's vision splendid."

"I was only fourteen and he broke on me like the Pacific
on stout Cortez. Lady Spencer's nephew! We'd heard so
much about him. All to his credit."

"Over a quarter of a century ago, Mitty. What harm to
talk about it? I like peaks in Darien."

"As you say, where's the harm? What's love at fourteen?
It was spring, the beguiling spring of adolescence, full of
immortal longings and infinite yearnings. I first saw him in
church, our church, remember? Easter was in April that year
—proud-pied April. Yes, it was on Easter Day—all those years
ago—in another world."

"It's always best," said my aunt, "to begin at the beginning."

CHAPTER 5

Easter Sunday!

The Peters family at full strength trooped into the second,
right-hand pew. Mother wore a confection of cyclamen veil-
ing. What a pretty woman she was! Father had a flower in his
buttonhole. Between them, we were arranged in order of
age, unless, of course, Geoff and I behaved unsuitably and
had to be separated.

I noticed he was already taller and much broader than
Martin, who was pale, even sallow, and slightly built. I al-

ways thought he had an old, worn look. His eyes? Slanted like a foreign cat's, yellow, wary and calculating. I saw him inspect my hat and his lips twitched, a little up to one side. I wanted to kick him. It wasn't my fault. Mother had insisted on daisies and forget-me-nots again—and I nearly grown up.

It wasn't in my nature to be resentful for long. The daffodils in the church were like corrugated sunbeams tucked in the old, grey stonework. Mother's pulpit was even more tasteful than usual. The organ filled the scooped-out hollows with splendid, reverberating sounds. The first hymn.

Alleluiah! Alleluiah! Al-le-lu-yah!

Geoffrey released his new baritone, shaky but impressive. I warbled ecstatically beside him.

Lady Spencer never got to church on time. She habitually lost a glove or laddered a stocking at the last minute—we'd hear her wails as we passed the house! Shouts of praise and joy were outbursting, *fortissimo,* as she entered, breathless after some fearful crisis. No one took any notice, of course, but the boy at her heels could not know that.

His hair was gold as the daffodils and he was blushing self-consciously. It made his eyes even bluer. I'd never seen anything so beautiful. I held my breath with astonishment and stopped singing altogether. For at that moment, at first sight, an arrow lodged in my waking heart, and truth to tell, felt singularly uncomfortable. Titania had not so prejudiced an eye for Bottom. Between one Alleluiah and the next, I fell in love.

"A new Heaven and a new Earth," the Vicar said. I saw exactly what he meant. There is something very elevating about a surrendered heart. There was I, wedged between Geoff and Peg, an adolescent monster, dowdy and ill-kempt, realizing I was older than Juliet and equally ready for the fray. Some small part of me grew up then, leaving the rest

more vulnerable. It didn't occur to me to think of John as a
boy. The archangel Gabriel would have impressed me less.
Geoff's whisper, therefore, came like a bucket of water.

"So that's *my dear nephew!*" He always chatted during the
canticles. "Looks a bit precious. What golden waves! Permed
do you think?"

"Shh!" Luckily this came from Peg, for I was speechless.
Already my loyalties threatened to tangle. Geoff and I never
disagreed about people and this new departure opened an
ugly gulf.

"He's not too bad," I shrugged at last; but my deceit
nearly choked me.

But the secret was not mine for long. Sonnets, one hundred
and thirty-two of them, I wrote at school and so no one could
see, but Martin spotted my starry gaze and I became a family
joke. Only Geoff was annoyed. I decided he was jealous. By
imputing the wrong motives to him, I insulted him for the
first time, for he was an utterly generous person. And we were
growing apart. While I struggled alone with my romance
Geoff was becoming a young man. It was he who made me
believe we were on the edge of war.

"Is that why you think of nothing but flying?"

"Not really. I love it for its own sake. But I don't pretend
it's only a hobby." He had already joined the air force.
"You're going to be reasonably pretty," he went on graciously,
"so you better learn how to behave, and with other chaps.
Brandon won't do you much harm, but the sooner you snap
out of that business the better."

"I love him," I replied with what I hoped was dignity.

"Don't be silly. Have you no sense? He's weak and con-
ceited and far too pretty-pretty."

But like many tomboys I was a loyal soul and despised
fickleness. I had left school, passing all the fashionable ex-
aminations. Father refused to allow his daughters to leave

home or take jobs. So it was essential to be athletic and easy
to be frivolous.

It was a lovely summer. Nineteen thirty-nine. I've never
seen such blossom. The apple trees were a pink froth all
around the lawn. I have never quite understood why I took
up with Martin. Geoff and I had never liked or trusted him.
I suppose he flattered my new adult mood, though I knew he
never did anything without a reason, and he moved in the
same circles as John. That was enough reason, I suppose.

The sun ripened a generous crop of apricots and Minnie
and I decided to bottle them. Minnie was a survival. It was
her second generation of domesticating the Brandons. She
was passionately attached to Father and patronized Mother.
It was my good fortune I was her pet. She was wise
and shrewd and when I complained of not having enough
to do she frightened Mother with a picture of my fate if I
never married, or if I did, and the result was I had to do the
cooking when the cook left and learn shorthand and typing.
I was to bless Minnie later.

My world grew more and more and more enclosed. I wal-
lowed in the hazy, physical well-being which sometimes fol-
lows breakdown, luxuriating more and more in remem-
brance of things past. It was so much easier to shelve the nagging prospect of the future. I had been caught in the right
mood, strong enough to reminisce indefinitely, weak enough
to be utterly suggestible. I began to know a voluptuous pleasure in confession.

In the daytime, it was very quiet, so I slept and slept, only
to wake alert at evening, ready for my aunt's company. To
avoid repetition of my two o'clock insomnia, she sat with me
till all hours, half-dozing in her armchair like a great, over-
dressed watchdog. Dreamily I picked up my story.

The third of September. Nothing prepares you for the

event, you must live through the experience. We had talked glibly for months, even years, but we thought of bombs and soldiers. We could not anticipate the state of mind, the climate of the inevitable. We expected air raids but faced evacuees, alien roundups, and canteen baked beans. Just as well.

The weather had been hot, almost sticky. I had been busy late the night before, helping Mother with preliminary billeting in the village. On the morning of the third, I went, after an early breakfast, to bask by the river. I felt self-conscious and guilty, expending what might be my last hours on earth in defiant sun-worship. Time went by, and the water looked more and more tempting. I put on my cap and headed in.

I was, of course, a strong swimmer, and had played on that particular reach since childhood. I kept carefully to the central channel and crawled energetically upstream. When I came to the bend, Lady Spencer was standing beside the water, her fat, pink face screwed up into misery, and tears coursing down her puffy cheeks. I had no idea what politeness required of me. I said, "Good morning."

She came back from some tremendous distance.

"The Prime Minister was on the wireless," she announced irrelevantly: "It's come!"

The shock was special, almost physical in its nature. I opened my mouth and dropped like a stone. Because my eyes were still open, I noted the water was a dirty yellow colour, very opaque. As there was no breath in my body I gulped the river before I realized what I was doing. I could still hear Lady Spencer's voice, see her old face, wrinkled into undignified tragedy. War! *It's come!* Death. Fear. Doubtful glory. Up to then, hope had lingered.

My feet were already entangled in the weeds and silt pushed up between my toes like toothpaste-ribbon. By all rules, it was time for panic. It didn't come. What, after all, was so terrifying about death by drowning? It was clean— and conventional.

I recall this oddly thoughtful interlude at the bottom of the river, for I was always to remember it; indeed, later it gained a more important implication than war itself. How long did it last? Physiology demands that it was brief. Yet during that time, I considered bombing, gassing, bacteriological warfare, only to pass beyond them to the two fundamentals of nature. All living things are plagued by the will to survive and the urge to reproduce themselves. To turn aside from these is to invite perversion.

Reduced to essentials, I kicked viciously and dislodged myself. I surfaced and gulped the upper air. I felt years older. Yet Lady Spencer was still standing at the bottom of her garden, apparently unaware of my temporary departure.

"I had two brothers killed last time," she was saying.

But I had only one who mattered!

When I reached home, I was still pinpointing essentials; I had proved the will to live, but what of reproduction, hitherto only a blur in biology lessons? Kill off one lot of people and you need more humans to replace them. To produce them was now the first requirement of girls in my age-group. In the days that followed, the most unlikely people proposed to me. But even a World War did not quell my romanticism.

It must have been tea time when John arrived.

"Let's go out, Mitty, and get away from everybody."

"I'd love that. Father's gone back to Ypres, Mother's got through all her handkerchiefs, and Peg has started knitting."

"It'll be over by Christmas," he said.

"I wonder. Geoff says we haven't nearly enough airplanes, and you should hear Martin on the top brass."

"Martin's here?"

"Heavens no! Nor will be till he decides on his niche. How about you, John? Heard anything?"

"I'll probably hang round here for a while, but you never know. Nothing's certain any more. Nothing." His voice shocked me. It was unsteady. The males of our family insisted on stiff upper lips.

The only advice I would give a girl in love is to guard against pity, which has a habit of sticking fast and dominating the complex. Nature, for better or worse, has made men in the shape of leaders. Shorn of their arrogant initiative, they confuse both their womenfolk and themselves.

That evening, my feelings toward John changed substantially, and the desire of the moth for a star converted itself into vaguely maternal superiority. I was too silly, too confused to understand this at the time, and if I felt mildly disappointed, I was flattered too. The new background besides bred noble, selfless standards, temporarily at least. Johnny had been my idol for four long years; the war threw him surprisingly into my grasp. It was my chance; I took it.

Within the week, we were engaged. Hasty marriages were the order of the day, and spirits were rising. There was no real opposition. Father preferred a married daughter to a Servicewoman, and gave his consent if I promised not to play camp-follower. My womenfolk loved a wedding. The interlude was sunny as the weather. John looked well in khaki and regained self-confidence. He was not a particularly urgent lover but I myself was shy and inexperienced. We appeared to agree on every point, I forget how.

I was still in love with love, or rather my own image of it, and was not very wise. It was subjective idealism adapted to holocaust.

Geoff came on leave later, and shook me a little out of position. He wore wings and flew Hurricanes. Strange, we'd hardly heard the name then! I remember greeting him with an excitement I reserved for Geoff alone. He was like a rock; normal, quiet and full of authority. It was as if the whole conduct of the war rested on his broad shoulders, and he was unperturbed as Atlas. No nostalgia, no heroics about my younger brother. He had been born, reared, dedicated to one end. He was a warrior, adjusted to battle.

"Why are you in such a hurry, Mitty? It's going to be a hell of a long war and there will be a lot of widows. Why get yourself involved with the rough when there's no hope of the smooth? I know you've got a crush on Brandon, but you choose a husband for keeps. Damn all sentimentality! Do you think you owe him something because he's cannon-fodder? Anyhow, when did he ever see a cannon?"

"You never did like Johnny."

"Any reason why I should?"

"Well, I do."

"He's not good enough for you."

"That's for me to decide. I don't much care about the distant future. Perhaps there won't be any. We've to live in the present whether we like it or not, and I'm marrying John with that in mind. It's logical—and there's never been anybody else. You've got to admit it."

"He's Martin's friend. That should put you off for a start."

"You go on and on about Martin."

"Of course I do. I don't like his social circle. And why? Because as Peters Minor I broke my nose my first term to protect my family name. And what Martin was at school, he still is. Vicious young brute."

"Schoolboys!" I shrugged. "Nasty little beasts! Anyhow, John's not Martin."

"You're right there. Hasn't his guts, his ingenuity, or his ability. The thing is—what *has* he got, bar those rather sissy good looks?"

"You're just trying to spoil everything!" I was miserable, angry, and childish.

"I wish I could! How much is there to spoil? The orange blossom soon dies. What's left over? Wake up, Mitty! You go through life wanting the *astra* without the *ardua*. And you'll land yourself in a first-class mess with a fifth-rate person. Hell! I'm wasting my time!"

Why did I make it so difficult for him? I hope he knew he came first, and I never expected John to be his equal. He was part of me, Geoff, and his dangers made the fates of others almost irrelevant. All this, I recognized instinctively, and because of it perhaps fought for my independence—a defense mechanism. It was as if I had a premonition of disaster, and plotted to have alternatives available. Or is that being wise long after the event? No matter. At the end of September, I was married.

The early-English church was decorated in autumnal colours where the daffodils had once made so brave a show. For a last time, we were a family, a community. Peters, Brandons, Spencers. The whole village, neighbourhood, county. I think of it as a requiem mass for a departed era.

I became Mrs. Brandon.

CHAPTER 6

As time went by, my doctor was more satisfied with my progress than my analyst. She had done very well but we were approaching rough ground. I resisted her.

"Pornography is so fashionable these days," she declared. "Let's have some intimate marital talk."

"Not from me," I replied. "Henry Miller can do what he likes. I haven't a clinical vocabulary."

"But you were reasonably happy at first?"

"I was reasonable. It isn't the same thing. I must have read a book by Havelock Ellis or something. I was disappointed by my honeymoon, but not particularly surprised. I think Mother told me life wasn't a bed of roses, nor Rome built in a day. I wasn't ill-informed."

"I'm glad to hear it."

"One thing about beds, you can always go to sleep in them. What really worried me was the stilted nature of our companionship. It was deteriorating rather than improving. We felt very awkward together. Even so, I imagine that's common too. Honeymoons are very artificial really. And one thing about mine; it ended, not in bliss, but in pregnancy.

"I'm a maternal beast, and it made me happy in a way. Yet I was worried too. It came on me so quickly; it stemmed from dissatisfaction; and it occurred to me, rather belatedly it was a poor world to offer a child. Never mind, I adjusted, and, on balance, I was content."

The circumstances were in my favour. Living at home, I hardly noticed I was married. John was posted up north. I was bursting with health and took a baby in my stride, and moreover when Minnie found a part-time munition job, I had more than enough to keep me occupied.

John didn't seem to have leave often, but Geoff was stationed nearby and got home more than usual.

"Still in a hurry." He grinned when he heard the news. "You remind me of a charging rhino."

"It's the thing to do," I replied amiably.

If I recognized that the incandescent quality of love was escaping me, I explained it away. It was irrelevant to domestic felicity, as one knew it. I was on the way to being a parent, and everyone knew how *dull* parents were.

"You can be godfather." I changed the subject hastily. "You'd better start saving up."

We were close together again. Geoff was never one to argue against the inevitable. John was my husband: it was necessary to hope for the best.

"Happy, Mitty?" he'd asked sometimes, and I would nod, forgetting it was because he was with me. We never imposed strain on each other. We could quarrel or laugh as the mood took us.

The war grew older. We were surprised when the stalemate ended. Little Geoffrey was born into a chaotic world. I remember Mother was more preoccupied with the safety of her Dresden collection than my ordeal. She had herself produced four children in close sequence, and thought nothing of it. I don't think she cared for being a grandmother at first, though she was glad it was a boy.

He was the best, the most special, the prettiest creature ever to be born. He gave me a sort of peace which no one could puncture. John, visiting me soon after, was far more dubious.

"Do you think he's all *right?*" he asked warily.

"All right? He's the most beautiful baby! Everyone says so."

"He's very fair."

"Why shouldn't he be? He takes after you."

"He'd look better if he were dark."

Mother said that was typical of a man, and obviously we thought the comment funny rather than odd. It must have been about that time that we had one of our rare conversations about marriage in general. I remember she gave me some advice about how to handle new fathers. It didn't apply, but she meant well. In exchange, I sounded her tactfully on the facts of life.

"Girls like you expect magic," she said. "I don't say it doesn't exist, but it doesn't last either. What matters is that John's a nice boy and we've known his family for years. You could have done much worse."

She was wrong.

How wrong was not yet manifest. The only unheeded warning at this time was the quarrel about the baby's name. I was determined to call him Geoffrey after his godfather. Equally, I was determined not to name him after Martin. John continued to argue by letter. Of course, I won.

Geoff was the one person in my life I have never needed to apologize for. When I think of him it's summer again; the last of it.

One day, I remember in particular. Geoff had the baby out under the trees. They lay side by side, asleep on a rug. I noticed with surprise that Geoff's hair was darkening, and lay flat and limp. A slight frown lingered between his eyes, his mouth drooped wearily, and two deep furrows scored his cheeks. Although he was brown, his tan concealed pallor, not ruddiness. He hadn't bothered to change into civilian clothes, and his uniform was not a clear, bayonet blue any longer. Only his D.F.C. looked fresh and clean, new as the phrase of war in the air.

"Geoff!" I called softly, and he opened his eyes and smiled at me lazily.

"Hello there! Come to keep us company?"

He had a friendly passion for his nephew whom he petted like a puppy or a kitten, and the baby was always good with him, as though he understood.

"Were you in town this morning? I missed you."

"I went in to see old Burgess."

"He's falling to pieces with age. What on earth for?"

He didn't answer at once. He looked at the boy. "I've made a will in Junior's favour. I like him and he likes me. Originally, I left everything to you, but I'm insured pretty heavily, and you can have the income. You may have other kids of course, but I fancy this one."

"I wish you wouldn't talk about wills."

"Silly Mittens!" he said quietly. "Do you expect me to last for ever? There's a certain payment attached to being a bloody hero and I'm not jibbing at it. And as I'm fighting for you and this creature, I might as well subsidize you as well. I'm not grumbling. Why should you?"

"I hate to hear you speak like that!"

"Head in the clouds, as usual! You always did believe what you wanted to be true. Far better to keep your two feet on the ground. Easiest way to stay upright. I want to talk to you, Mitty, because it's time you started thinking about things like money. This child's got to be reared. I'm making my contribution, but see that John makes his too, well in advance. He's a feckless chap with pretty extravagant tastes. Secondly—don't rely on Father. The parents have lived above their income for years and will feel a pretty appalling draught before they're much older. Already a lot of their foreign stock is worthless. Never trust money you can't feel between your fingers. Never rely on anyone but yourself. If anything happens to me, you may well find yourself out on a limb. Keep your head, and keep your balance. Here endeth the lesson. I doubt if the part of preacher suits me. Let's be more jolly! Do you feel like a pub-crawl?"

Minnie put the baby to bed and we went out. The old car still hung together, precariously as the world about us. We drank rather more than usual, and commented on it.

"That's another thing," Geoff said. "Keep John off the alcohol."

"What a nerve!" I exploded. "He's temperate, compared with you!"

Geoff grinned, but his eyes held no humour. "He drinks spasmodically and holds it badly, whereas my head is like a rock. And I know when to stop. Don't be angry with me, Mitty. Not tonight. I only want you happy."

"I'm happy," I protested.

"It won't hurt you to toughen up. You're a big girl now. And meanwhile keep John off the hard liquor and brother Martin's company. He's evil, Mitty. Awkward word, but the only repeatable adjective that describes him. Look out for him, if anything happens to me. He loses no love where you're concerned."

"I wish you wouldn't keep talking about. . . ."

"Getting killed? It happens every day in a Fighter Squadron. All right, idiot. Don't look so woebegone! I may survive. Frankly, I'd rather like to, given the chance."

His hand covered mine. I looked away. There was a row of pewter mugs. They grew very blurred.

He went back next morning. I saw him off, and if, when he had rounded the corner, I felt ice-cold—well! It was often like that. I always hated saying goodbye to Geoff.

One week . . . two . . . then it happened. Mother and I were in the drawing room. There was a concert on the wireless. Dvorak's Fourth was a favourite of mine. I could never stomach it afterwards.

The doorbell rang. We had forgotten that it had by the time Father came in. He was holding a telegram. He looked very old and bewildered, his eyes pleading. But when he spoke, his voice was quite cold and expressionless.

"They're giving him a Bar to his D.F.C.—posthumously," he said.

Mother began to cry horribly, trembling all over.

I walked out of the room.

They had their levels of grief; I had mine. They had their cures; I had none. They had each other; I had no one. Geoff was dead.

But I was young and resilient. I had a child and a husband. My disregard of John in crisis had scared me. Belatedly, I was guilty. I'd have traded him for Geoff, you see. But now my whole attitude had changed. I didn't want to do or feel anything I might regret.

I never did cry for Geoff. It was the last tribute I could pay him. He had always been impatient with tears, so it was appropriate to mourn him dry-eyed. I did not know then that toughness is dangerous. My adjustment was slow, but sure. The baby, the routine, helped. The sun still rose every morning and each month brought a new, sickle moon.

John wrote me a scrappy letter of condolence and kept out of the way, so I could recover without his assistance. Not that I wanted to discuss Geoff with him, or anyone else, but I noticed he didn't even try. Martin did come home and cheered Mother up enormously. To hear him talk to Father, you'd have thought the whole conduct of the war was in his hands, but as far as I could see, he was doing as little as possible in the safest place he could find. I told him so.

"Quite right, little sister. Why not?"

"You might write to Mother more regularly. Even a postcard from you gives her pleasure. You should write at least once a week."

"What on earth about? Nothing to report in my benighted existence. I am far too old to write home-letters like a scruffy preparatory schoolboy. One advances."

"In the wrong direction," I snapped.

A favourite dream was to supply Geoffrey with a little sister, and imagine them playing together, as we had done. When John came home, I daresay this was in the back of my mind, and anyhow, I found sex a drug and an antidote. I was much more physically mature and demanded my rights. The answering lack of warmth was shaming, but I braved it like a drunkard who postpones the hangover. Maybe I couldn't have coped just then with tenderness, so it was as well I didn't find it.

It was a very short leave. It left a very bad taste. I could no longer persuade myself that my marriage was going in the right direction. So what to do about it? The onus seemed to be on me, and its study a sort of mental exercise. Marriage guidance experts are very glib. "Talk it over together," they say. Have they ever tried? Lovers can say nearly anything. Friends well outside the physical bracket can discuss a great deal. But in an unbalanced relationship, the silence is the worst part of the frustration.

I did my best. I had one suggestion. Love-making at home, or at Lady Spencer's, had an odd smack of immorality. In the freer, less inhibited atmosphere of London, we could start again and probably do better. John liked the idea. He had a Fourteen Days due, almost any moment, he said.

I arranged extra help with the baby, and planned my emancipation with enormous pleasure. I was optimistic and excited. After all, I was only nineteen, and lately life had been dull as well as unhappy. The day came and it was like Christmas, Easter, and school Speech Day, all rolled into one. Everything seemed possible that brave morning in early autumn—even happiness.

I was alone in the hall when the telegram came. I handled it fearfully and for a coward moment wanted to go to Father and delegate the job. If I had? But there is never any guarantee that a different life would be a better one. I tore it open.

It cancelled all arrangements. John's leave had been called

off. No other explanation. I was annoyed. He might have telephoned to explain. Perhaps he thought nothing of it, but I did. All my beautiful hopes called off too!

My hands worked independently. First, I screwed up the paper, then, seeing what I had done, I recognized the rightness of the reflex. I had chosen to go out of mourning; I had planned to start again, Mitty Brandon, rather than Geoff's young sister. What did it matter if John were not available? I could have my fun alone; I liked my own company. I said nothing to the family and caught the train I had intended.

CHAPTER 7

I had taken a good deal of trouble over my appearance; I had a chronic, confiding smile glued to my face; even strangers in the train were cheered by my presence. I was like a damned ray of sunshine.

I reached London. How enormous it always looks after absence! I lost a little of my bounce and grew confused. It had been left to John to find accommodation and look after the practical side. Were the hotels very full? Which should I choose? Which theaters and restaurants were open? What else to do in a Blitz?

The sirens helped me. I had no intention of trudging round in an air raid, lugging a heavy suitcase. Mother had given me the spare key to Martin's flat, which was not far from the terminus. When I found not even a taxi was available, I decided to walk there. I could dump my luggage, use his telephone, and search for a room in comfort.

It was still quiet when I gained the shelter of the entrance hall. I tucked my luggage under the bannisters and faced the long flight of stairs. I didn't intend to stay there. It was a convenient, temporary measure. There were a lot of stairs and I climbed them too quickly. On the second landing, I paused, feeling dizzy. My scanty breakfast? Fear of the approaching raid, controlled and not quite manifest? Or a possible new baby?

Whatever the cause, the effect soon passed, though I climbed the last flight more cautiously and rested again at the top. I found the key. The door opened noiselessly. The hall was a mere alcove off the sitting room. It was a small flat.

I knew at once I was not alone. Martin used a very distinctive hair oil. The place reeked of him. It was still quiet outside, no guns, no airplanes. London waited in silence and so did I. Their voices carried through the thin walls. Martin, in particular, was audible. He had a trained voice and clipped his consonants like an actor. I shivered.

I don't know how I dared to register and analyze. I suppose, at first, it was unreal or I shouldn't have lingered. People didn't use some words, not in that way, so they hit, almost ripped the stretched surface of the ear drum. What was this? What had Geoff said? Hadn't he warned me? But it was hard to believe such things happened. A girl of my generation had no concern for by-ways, areas of human filth outside my comprehension. But not, surely not, within my own family? I wouldn't, *couldn't* accept them. It was too utterly horrible!

And then I understood. The other voice was familiar too. Not just Martin, my brother, but John, my husband.

Shock hit me without pity. I froze like a dead thing. I daren't move, breathe. I didn't have to think. I knew what was going to happen. The bedroom door opened.

He didn't see me, motionless pillar of salt that I had become. John didn't see me. I've always been grateful for that. He looked quite different, irradiated, touched by some wand of depravity, oddly virile. He walked over to the window, while Martin stalked him, elegantly as a leopard with a blood-lust. Martin! He wore his amused, almost feline expression of triumph. The devil himself would have been less impressive.

Nowadays they think of Sodom and Gomorrah as hot night-spots, and you'll often take a book at random out of a library which instructs you sympathetically about men involved with men. What I have never seen is an account of the reactions of a normal, breeding woman, confronted with anti-nature; of a young, uncomplicated child admitting her husband belongs to a different species. Not that I need enlightenment. The horror and shock is with you all your life. Repair the damage, but still the joins show.

Martin and John! *John!* He had touched me, taken me—for better or for worse. But not . . . not, dear God! for this!

I tried not to listen. I tried not to look. They'd involved me in their filthy travesty of humanity. My skull pressed on my brain. It hurt.

They returned as they'd come. Somehow I found myself safely in the street. The guns had started; there was shrapnel; bombs too, I suppose. I don't know. I can't remember what happened. Later I found a ticket for left luggage. I must have been sleepwalking when I checked it in. Odd I should have crossed the borders of sanity, and have forgotten what it was like.

Traumatic shock, I believe they call it. I read about it once. Mine had varying degrees of intensity. It came . . . it went. I next found myself slinking along as though hell pursued me. In what direction? Did it matter? All paths led out of Eden. I had eaten of the tree of knowledge and its poison spread inexorably, paralyzing my soul till it shrivelled and could no longer impel me.

I was next roused by a woman in a tin helmet, who ordered me under cover. As if it mattered! Up till then the pandemonium of the raid had been an irrelevant orchestration, uninteresting as discordant film music, and just as pointless. Only memory was real, lethal, unescapable. I'd watched a house crumble like a cake, and thought nothing of it. I nearly explained I was trying to get killed, and that it was better to do so than try the job myself. But when I opened my mouth, no words came. None at all. I tried again. Same result. I'd been struck dumb!

It was awkward. Not vitally important, but awkward. My breakdown was evidently complete, but there were no known onlookers, and it might prove temporary. The first duty of madness is to conceal it. I appeared cooperative.

As soon as the woman had gone, I dodged out of sight, slipping along side streets stealthily, till I found myself in a park. To this day, I have no idea which one. I lay back gratefully on its harsh, grimy grass and the first leaves of autumn drifted over me.

Thought was dull and slow. Only the scene in the flat was etched corrosively on my brain; even the raid could not drown those echoing, intimate voices.

He couldn't be my husband; he *couldn't!* He wasn't the father of my son! The sins of fathers visited on little children. And not only babies. Mother, gentle and ignorant, loving Martin absurdly. Father, actually proud of him! They were still in Eden, but unguarded by angels.

Geoff would know what I must do. But, no! Geoff was dead.

If the raid didn't kill me, I couldn't kill myself. I remembered the bottom of the river at home. Well, I'd reproduced

myself, and now against my will, I must live for my reproduction, if only I could manage to live with myself—and
John!

It was impossible, *impossible!* But how could I shake him
off? You couldn't stand up with everybody looking on, face a
divorce court, say your husband had jilted you for your
brother! Dirt smeared everywhere. Children's heritage tarnished; Mother devastated; you couldn't write it on the wall
for all to see. So what was left? Silence, endurance, horror.
Even the luxury of self-blame was denied me. I had done
nothing wrong. I was just an ignorant plaything of a fate, who,
personified, ruthless and cruel, looked extraordinarily like
Martin.

Martin! Here only I could grip and grasp. I *hated* him.
It was better than the cold despair which made it impossible
to think about John with comprehension and continuity.
Martin had always been cunning, decadent and deliberately destructive. He was evil; he was dangerous. He out-
classed me as a fighter. Bitten, he would bite. For the sake of
the vulnerable folk, I must risk no mistakes.

So I stopped thinking of murder.

I was surprised to find myself still talking to Aunt
Anglesey. I had almost believed myself back in that day in
London. The late hour, the unbroken concentration allowed
me to retrace the desolation of that pathetic nineteen-year-
old facing a life which could never be mended. For there was
no solution. Even death could not cancel the scene in Martin's flat. I still searched the faces of my children for signs of
their unfortunate breeding—and sometimes I thought I saw
them.

"Child—why didn't you come to me? You could have
trusted me."

"I trusted no one, and rightly so."

"We could at least have talked."

"I tell you, I couldn't speak. You don't pay social calls when your tongue seems to have been cut out. I wasn't able to ask for a cup of tea, or a drink."

"I had no idea things were as bad as this. And you told no one?"

"I shouldn't have told you now. I wish I hadn't. I made a solemn vow. Oddly enough—in a church."

It wasn't much of a church really. The roof had gone and there was rubble round the altar. Very appropriate. I found myself there, quite accidentally, shivering and crouching on the chancel steps after another blank period. I was remembering my wedding, not with masochism, but with bewilderment. The law could not offer me divorce, but what of Heaven, in whose name the mistake was made?

I believed in God, but couldn't reach Him. People in Hell can't. Yet there seemed sense in putting forward my case. He didn't need speech. Everyone else did. He would understand I'd made my marital promises in ignorance and simplicity. It was necessary to exchange one set of promises for another, and see they were fair to everyone. I now rededicated myself to Geoffrey; to my parents' honour; to the burial of my pride. Old loyalty was cancelled; a new interpretation laid down. If I had things to live for, I had nothing to live by. And my brain began to give way again.

After I left the ruined church, everything goes blank again. I next remember the velvety, impenetrable dark of the black-out with a bomber's moon above, obscured by flying clouds. I was suddenly conscious of physical discomfort. I had walked for miles; I had nothing to eat all day. My head ached and waves of exhausted nausea swept over me. I was lost. Only the sky was alive; smooth pencil-searchlights, blinding flashes, a dull red glow to the west.

Some time in the early hours, the All Clear sounded and soon after a man shone a torch on my face. I think of him as a seaman, for he had a beard and they weren't often worn. He was drunk, I believe. He grabbed hold of me.

I doubt if I were really afraid. I was beyond normal reactions. I wasn't shocked. He had a right to accost a lone girl streetwalking at such an hour. But that a *man* should actually touch me, breathe on me. I couldn't stand it! I should have felt the same with a policeman or a doctor. It was unbearable. I started to scream.

Until that moment, I hadn't understood how I'd worried about my voice. The emerging sound pushed me to ecstasy and exhilaration. I couldn't stop. I felt like a prima donna triumphant on a top note. On, on and on! I could sustain it forever! The spell was broken. I could move forward again.

At the end of my fortnight, I went home. It was interesting to realize my experiences were not stamped indelibly on my face. In the glass, I myself saw a stranger, but no one else did. I knew once and for all what it was like to be a changeling.

"You look well on a chaise longue," my aunt remarked next day, "and I have admirable taste in negligée. You're still a pretty woman, if you'd take a little trouble. I must think you over and plan your renaissance."

"Terrifying thought!" I laughed. "But thank you for this dressing gown. How wonderful it is to be convalescent."

"I know just the person to style your hair. We'll make you charming and devastate George—and any other man we can find."

"Middle-aged charm requires infinite leisure—and money," I pointed out cheerfully.

"I should say serenity was more important, and we're nearer that than we were."

"With you biting like a gadfly? Still, I must admit, your methods pay off. I feel better for my brainwashing. Though I'm glad it's over."

"Is it? Thanks to my grit, tact and determination, we progress well, but don't think you can wriggle off the hook. There are many gaps to fill, too many for comfort."

"Do you want every day of my life?"

"No—only thirteen of them."

"But I'd just got back to the Grange," I countered hastily, "and Heaven knows there was enough going on there."

"Very well. Later."

Now I could float through the days with an increasing feeling of well-being, and even take in my family when they called. Geoff came to tell me he was thinking of sharing rooms with a friend in London, and working harder. Mother had evidently disposed of the toothy Helga. She told me so with gentle pride when she came with Renata and Peg. My daughter actually liked my young sister's husband, a narrow but kind businessman with only one warmth and that for his childless wife whom he trained to be part angel, part goddess, and part status symbol. Now the vacation chores of dentist and uniforms were finished, Ren begged to be allowed to visit Peg for the remainder of the time, to go to a dance, and to borrow my star sapphire pendant. By this time a little weary, I agreed to everything. Even Mike arrived one morning early to announce he was going climbing in the Cairngorms, to eat my breakfast and depart with what money was in my pocketbook. After these visitations Aunt Anglesey was almost a relief. Also that night I had had another long nap.

"You had just returned to the Grange," she reminded me.

She didn't need to. My life was unreeling itself all too clearly. . . .

At home I found that Father had had a slight stroke and was in the hospital, Mother at his side. No word had come in my absence from either Martin or John. No one was interested in me; I might get away with my deception. Father came home, grumbling miserably, on the arm of a Mother suddenly frightened and insecure. A postcard arrived from Martin telling that he had been sent abroad. Somewhere from her own misery Mother took a moment to notice me. She accepted my quite dreary condition when I told her another baby was on the way and was vaguely reassured at my assurance that an evacuated specialist at the hospital was looking out for me. Second babies could account for anything for Mother.

John didn't come near me after Martin went abroad; he was posted to Scotland and of course everyone thought we'd been on leave in London. I pulled myself together gradually and went off to meet him at a half-way house, a dismal Yorkshire pub. Instead of any of the many meetings I had envisioned, I found myself nurse and my marital duties reduced to taking care of him and his shocking cold. I thought him ludicrous rather than repulsive. Only then could I bring myself to speculate about John and face my dilemma. I believed that though John might have formed his curious tastes at school there wasn't much wrong with him at the time of our wedding. But he had cheated in choosing me. I was hampered by my vanity. I'd loved him. What sort of a fool did it make me? I was a dogged girl, but it took me a long time to be clear-sighted.

Then everything was swallowed up by Michael's birth. I was very ill and my evacuated specialist proved a real friend. At home they had no idea how bad things were, for Father had had another mild stroke. My planning was easier because Mike was the worst baby ever. Only Minnie was dubious about my moving to Scotland. "You'll never manage on your own with those two. This new one's a tartar. And you do look poorly."

I was never to live at the Grange again. The Ministry commandeered the house and built Nissen huts on the tennis lawn. Not that it mattered; no one remembered how to play anymore.

So, after a series of dismal lodgings, we went to the unoccupied croft at Achnawhinnie. The Laird was glad to keep the place aired and tenanted at a nominal rent by someone who scorned luxury. I learned to pump water, trim oil-lamps, stack peats. But for the first time I gulped clean clear air, slept as much as I needed, forgot I had a worry, and began to feel human again. There may be more beautiful places, but not for me. I could sit for hours watching the changing colors of the hills or the rain-needles slanting against the wild winds. I've never known such peace, dropping slow, delicately healing, consoling as the spring's rebirth. My children felt it too, and laughed and grew fat.

The war dragged on but the high hills insulated us. John came now and then, reluctantly. As Geoff had warned me, he proved feckless and money grew difficult. I kept hens and grew vegetables and learned to watch every penny.

I won't pretend I was sorry when Martin was killed. I was surprised, however, that he could miscalculate. If I grieved it was for Mother. As for John, I hadn't appreciated how involved he'd been. He was a man unable to make satisfying human contacts. My brother alone had succeeded in igniting his spark and at his death it was extinguished. He had learned to worship Martin, who had the devil's own liking' for a stolen soul. Ironic I should understand. I never told him I knew. I was all he had left and I did what I could. With me now and again John could find Martin. Poor Renata! That was how she was born.

Father died, almost in debt. Peg married, apparently happily. John was put on active service. The front-line was no place for him, nor the base. When they threw him out of the army he began to drink. We came south and John lost job after job. Of course I thought of divorce, but he wouldn't have cooperated, or accept collusion: I was his last prop. I couldn't risk losing the children by taking matters in my own hands. Yes, I was very relieved when he died.

"But there were other men in the world, surely," broke in my aunt. The fire had lowered and her face was shadowed. "I have never known you to indulge in the faintest flutter. Do you hate men?"

"I don't think so."

"Then we must talk about the gap. We'll look at Michael again, for your own good and his too. You're not handling him properly, and it might be helpful to have some idea who his father was, that is, if you know yourself."

I stared at her incredulously. "If I know . . . ?"

"You may not. You said there in London you had lost your mind; you could have lost your memory. What were the dates of those missing thirteen days?"

"I can't remember."

"I'm now certain Michael isn't John's son, and that you never thought he was."

"I wasn't sure for ages. And does it matter? Life's a muddle; war's a muddle, and as for love, it's the worst goddam muddle of them all!"

"I'm just trying to bring you to the point, child."

"Which is Mike, always Mike. What right had I to give him that start? I've branded him. And you have guessed. While I could persuade myself I'd never be found out, there was hope. I feel like a criminal."

"Mitty, dearest child, I hadn't suspected this and it's taken me nearly a fortnight to bring you to this point. Can you

60

imagine I'll betray you? But there's only one person who could undo your work. Michael's father."

"He's dead. They killed him too. He never knew he had a son, nor Mike that I gave him so special a father. You sent on the letter, you know, readdressing it with my married name. I'd borrowed yours for that purpose. It came just before Mike was born. That's why I was so ill."

"Mitty, I want you to finish your tale. It's important for you and all your children. You've repressed everything too long. Go on. . . . There was a seaman with a beard. You were screaming. Start there. One day gone and thirteen more to come. Let's have it out of your system."

CHAPTER 8

A scream. A miracle of sound. The release of horror. Louder and louder, while I stood quite still. I had now lost power of movement and was inexorably enclosed in nightmare.

I remember the torch most clearly. It jerked away and fell; I saw it roll along the ground. Then, to my surprise, it lifted up, reverted, and shone on its owner's face. The man lay prone; his eyes were shut.

Mind hitched to body at last. I could speak. Moreover there was a sensual pleasure in words for words' sake.

"The Lord smote him in the midst of his wickedness. He can if He wants to. I wish all men lay in the gutter where they belong."

"Massacre on the grand scale. Macabre ideas." I assumed

the voice was in my own head, though its intonations were unfamiliar.

"Martin and John too. Down where he is. Dead; quite dead."

"He's drunk and out cold," the voice corrected.

"No! God struck him down. I saw it."

"No one has ever mistaken me for God before," the accent was strange, puzzling. "Let's say I'm a divine agent with a good right hook. And now, could we be less Old Testament and clear out before there's any further excitement?"

"You're real," I accused. "You're not a voice. I thought you were. It's difficult to tell. You see—I've gone mad."

"You do seem a trifle distrait. Have you been too near a bomb?"

"Not near enough," I replied. "It would have solved everything."

The torch was fading, shaken by its fall. I didn't mind the duller light on my face.

"Poor pretty Ophelia! You wear your rue with a difference! Let's start walking, shall we? My car's nearby. I hope it's still in one piece."

"It's funny. All day, I haven't been able to talk; now I can I'm rooted to the spot. I must have awful gaps in my brain. Anyhow, where could I go? Who could help me? Have you noticed they always kill the best people? Why should I live in the same world as John and Martin? But when you want death, it doesn't want you."

"The converse is equally true." I wondered why he should laugh. "But you know, you will feel better tomorrow; people do. I shall take you home with me. You'll be quite safe there."

"No! You'll ring up Father . . . you'll put me into a lunatic asylum. Why not? But I won't tell them anything . . . ever! I'll go dumb again, so I can't."

62

"You're tired and shocked and your teeth are chattering. You needn't talk at all. I'll heat you some milk, and light the fire. And you can rest comfortably. When did you last eat?"

"Breakfast, I suppose. Not much though. I was too excited. How could I guess it would end like this?"

"Come along," he said firmly. "I want to take a closer look at you, before I decide what's best to do. You can walk perfectly well if you want to."

"I can't," I shook my head miserably.

"Then I'll carry you. The sooner I get you warm, dry and fed, the sooner you'll feel human again."

He picked me up effortlessly and I laid my head naturally against his shoulder. It was impossible to be wary or critical. He used the same shaving soap as Geoff and this convinced me he was trustworthy. I was conscious of power and height and cleanliness. His voice was part of me and the darkness. It had a pretty lilt to it, very persuasive. I closed my eyes feeling extraordinarily safe and untroubled.

I remember nothing more of our journey.

Minutes, hours later, for there was still no definable passage of time, I noticed a gas fire. I'd never seen such a big one in my life; its very size brought back my wits.

I was in a large, essentially beautiful room. Its elaborate plasterwork was cracked, it was shabbily furnished, but its proportions were restful and satisfying. I wore a thick dressing gown, enormously large for me; I sat on an ancient sofa, pushed right up to the fire. I thought I'd go to sleep again.

"Drink this down." It was the voice again. I opened my eyes.

"I've made you a fearful mixture. I hope it's both medicinal and sustaining. I'll hold the glass. Fine! There's my girl! Now—don't you feel better already?"

It was my first opportunity to see him clearly. His face,

like his voice, was part of me. I found myself level with his eyes, knowing them, recognizing them.

"*Déja vu?*" I wondered aloud.

"Strange, isn't it?" His smile was so intimate it took my breath away. "I feel the same, incidentally."

I was still light-headed. It dissolved all the usual inhibitions. Prepared for delusions, I had to touch him to prove his reality. As I put out my hand, he caught it and laid it against his cheek in a quiet gesture of affection. And so we stayed, very still, just looking at each other. No words; there was nothing to say aloud. We asked each other a silent question; and answered it.

His smile was shy, tentative.

"Are you warm now? Would you like a decent drink? You can go to sleep, you know, if you like. You're safe with me. This is your asylum. I'll be your nurse. I think I probably was anyhow in some previous existence."

"Someone I valued very much certainly."

"Only valued?" he countered softly.

He was tanned, young, hard as whipcord, and his eyes were dark, slate-grey under level black brows. That smile was a flash of small, uneven teeth which dispersed itself into quizzical laughter lines, and called up a single, provocative dimple in his thin cheek. He was clean as the wind off the high eternal hills, beguiling as a favourite song. His special beauty for me was not measurable by ordinary words. It transcended common description.

"I'm glad I've met you," I said. "There's no point to it, but I'm glad."

He smoothed my hair away from my eyes. "What pretty curls! I'm glad too, love. I thought I could manage without you. I was wrong. It gives life new meaning, whether one wants it or not. How old are you?"

64

"Nineteen. And it's too late. I have a son and a husband. I'm sorry."

"I saw your wedding ring. Does it apply?"

"I hate him. I hate both of them!"

"Hush! John and Martin I suppose, damn them! Listen to me. We've found each other; that's enough for tonight."

"If it could only turn out to be a nightmare. If only I could wake up and find myself still free . . . then. . . ."

"Then?"

"I could love you so well. I do anyhow."

"That makes two of us, so we'll forget everybody else. Don't be afraid I'll harm you or involve you. There's not enough time. There's only now—a few hours at most."

"And so . . . ?" But I knew, really.

"Do you want cards on the table? A fortnight, three weeks, at best a month, and I shall be a pulse in the eternal mind, no less. And no great loss either."

"They killed my brother Geoff," I said. "They take the kind and good and leave the evil."

"It's what goes on, love. Life and death are wantons nowadays. There are compensations. Take you—the girl of a lifetime! I'll certainly love you till I die, think of that! Not many can say it with such ringing conviction. It hasn't happened before; it won't again. Idiot! Don't look so woebegone. You have the prettiest smile. Use it!"

"It's a horrible world," I cried.

"Nonsense! It's a bonnie world. When you're near to leaving it, you feel differently. The trees are beginning to change colour; the mornings have a sharp tang to them already. And soon it will be winter. Hoarfrosts will embroider the iron railings; the stars will be clear-cut, brilliant above the black-out. You'll be there. Waiting for spring . . . think of it! . . . winter over. As for the summer . . . do you know Scotland at all? I'd like to feel you were my proxy. Could see life, just as I do. It might make sense of our meeting. I've nothing else to give you."

"Stop it," I said. "Stop it!"

For answer he held out his arms, and we were suddenly where we belonged, protected from harm, ugliness and hurt. I could now cry without washing away my entity. At first, it was difficult; my sobs were rackingly dry. But he encouraged and steadied me, till there was relief and ease.

"That's better," he whispered. "Much better. Don't try and stop yet. I was afraid for you, darling. You'll be fine now." He stroked my head, twisting little tendrils of hair between fingers.

"Everything's right about you," he went on. "Who'd have thought I'd find someone just the best size for my shoulder; tailored to fit my arms? Oh, my very dear one—what are you doing to me? I only know I like it, *like* it—and no sense to it at all."

"Why did it have to happen this way?" I was still sobbing.

"Never you mind. Just cry your misery out of your system, so that for a little while, we can be happy together. Rather a high price, so we must get our value. Not that you aren't a very desirable commodity."

"Am I?"

"Yes indeed, love." He could laugh so softly, so intimately. "I wondered what I needed, and here you are. Do you know, I nearly got drunk tonight. Instead, I found you. This was meant to happen. Don't you feel that too? We suit each other's requirements."

I shook my head doubtfully, and nestling against him, cried on. Now and again, he mopped my eyes efficiently with a khaki handkerchief. Sometimes he murmured silly things; sometimes not. And then he kissed me very gently, very hes-

itantly, because neither of us at first could bear the beauty
of it.

"I didn't know it could be like this. Did you?"

"Glimpses in dreams perhaps. I could never see your
face."

"Is that why you *gaze*, so you can dream about me?"

"I don't want to dream," I said. "Life's better."

"Told you so, love. Now perhaps you'll believe me."

It was the final irony that I ended those twenty-four hours,
deeply content, and that I fell asleep like a child, suddenly
and naturally, curled in his arms.

A telephone bell woke me. I heard a man's voice,
clipped and decisive, talking in riddles. I wondered who he
could possibly be.

I gathered my wits slowly. Nothing was real but the sun,
silhouetting the tracery of an iron balcony beyond which
seemed to be Regent's Park with a silvery dew on it. Could
it really have happened to me? The horror? The beauty?

He came into the room, crossed over into a patch of sun-
light, and stood very still, looking down on the street. A
young man, clean-cut, erect, who held his head high. Resolute, even arrogant, he was almost unbearably attractive,
but too vital and vivid, surely, to be a hallucination?

Besides, he had a name, a name that matched him.

"Ronan," I murmured reminiscently. "Ronan."

As if I had called him, he came to me at once. I searched
anxiously for the remembered smile, but he was serious.

"Did the telephone wake you? Do you feel better? You
look more human this morning."

"I'm making a great nuisance of myself."

"Not at all. How could you? I love you, remember? Perhaps you've forgotten, or maybe want to forget."

"I thought it might be wishful thinking." I was awkward,
diffident.

"No, it's true—better and worse; but there's a new development. I've been given a reprieve. Departure delayed, ten days, a fortnight perhaps. So you see, it's a miracle of a day and a day for miracles. I can't believe it yet."

"Really? Truly? Oh, Ronan, it's a sort of eternity."

"We could make it so. Reduce time to hours, minutes, even seconds. But no—everything may look different to you this morning."

"You look the same, exactly."

"So do you. You're the loveliest thing I ever saw. I wish you weren't, so no one would ever appreciate you but me. You're what I've wanted always, only better."

He was smiling again.

He had an elegant nose, down-curved, symmetrical. I traced its contour with my index finger.

"So what do we do about it?" I inquired.

"You do realize, don't you, that it won't always be like last night. In other worlds, God willing! but not here. Don't think of me as a Galahad, now we've time on our side. It's only because I'm a man of principle that I don't make love to you before breakfast. Which reminds me, I'm hungry. Are you? How thoroughly unromantic!"

In the years ahead, when I would lie alone and remember him, I used feelings rather than facts for currency. To shut my eyes was to recall laughter, tenderness, companionship—drugs which banish loneliness for a short space. I would avoid those irrelevant things which most seemed to endorse his reality. He had a passion for marmalade; he whistled *Figaro* when he shaved; his hands might seem to caress me again, but if they adjusted the minute hand of his pale-faced clock, I could *see* them, long and brown with squared fingernails. I couldn't ever bear to think of them, changed, buried. I can't now.

He had a preoccupation with minutiae; he aimed at perfection in small matters as though he would dismiss all beyond his control. I remember him as a very efficient young man, well able to moor the drifting. I put myself in his charge and he dealt with me conscientiously, taking pleasure, deep pleasure, in his responsibility.

I run ahead. On that first morning, I was in love. Even eating had a sort of splendour. Everything was new, electrifying. My problems could not be solved, so I postponed them.

We washed up the breakfast things before he kissed me. How typical of Ronan! Then he made up for lost time, bless him!

"What shall I do wi' ye?" he teased.

"The same again?"

"My dearest on earth, we must be more solemn. Now, rather than later. It's all too obvious where this leads—and I really am a man of principle." He played with my left hand in silence.

"My marriage? It's less than nothing. It's a mess, Ronan. I can't escape. I might as well forget. Even before I met you, I'd rescinded all I promised. Don't think I'm a tramp. I'm rather a prig really. But what are principles? There's something obscene about living and dying John's property. That's what would be immoral. Dreadfully so. But I can't explain."

"But you intend to stay with him?"

"What else can I do? There's Geoffrey. There's Mother. No alternative. Perhaps you can learn to endure what you least tolerate, if the cause is good enough."

"Would you like me to judge? I know I'm prejudiced, but only indirectly involved. And love, you were half-mad last night, and who knows that you're rational this morning?"

I shook my head. "It's irrelevant. But if you want me, just take me, and to hell with it!"

"Darling, look at me! Of course I want you, but I'm not a poacher by inclination, nor as licentious as soldiery ought to be. Calvin lurks in me, if not something rather more primitive. Frankly, I'd prefer to knock your husband's teeth in and play this straight."

"Touch pitch," I shrugged, "and you'll be defiled too. As I am."

"Did you catch him out with another girl?"

I laughed bitterly. "I'd have got over that, you know. Or at least I could have divorced him. But this! I keep thinking of Mrs. Oscar Wilde. Uncle Peregrine knew her. The two boys had to change their name. Poor things."

"Oscar Wilde?"

"It's worse, you know. Martin's my brother. Thank God they didn't see me. And that they went back to bed."

"I see."

"I doubt it. But you did save my sanity, and you're entitled to some reward."

"That's no way to talk. No way at all. You don't owe me anything. I was bored and depressed, and knight errantry had a flavour of novelty."

"I'm sorry I had to tell you. But you see I'm his wife and part of his degradation. I'm not fit for anyone decent anymore."

He shook me roughly. "Don't dare to talk like that. I was only afraid you might come to regret this. I've nothing to lose, everything to gain. But I do love you; I don't want to cause you injury; finish off what others began. Having found my connoisseur's piece, I can't just steal it without so much as by your leave. For that's what you are, *m'eudail*. There you were, all dusty and tarnished among the rubbish, and I've taken you and cleaned you up like a prize find in a junk shop."

"You use the oddest similes!" I smiled as he intended. "And what on earth does *m'eudail* mean?"

"That my heart is highland, love, and you belong to me. Just the same, it was more straightforward when only a few hours were involved. Now it's a larger decision altogether. This isn't our country really, is it? I doubt if it's even a matter of whether I sleep on the bed or the sofa. If we use this gift of time and freedom, our relationship must be its own excuse, and anyhow, it's the expenditure of a lifetime in one mad burst."

"It'll work out. It must. We want the same things; have the same standards. Doubt seems ungracious."

"On then! And Calvin be damned! And having settled that, let's have some coffee. The heart must pause to breathe."

When I look back, our youth horrifies me. We were both shy, conventional people, who felt somewhat bareheaded as we tossed our bonnets over the windmill. Success dogged us, not because we were dedicated and high-minded, nor even because we were physical complements, but our moods and needs, synchronized perfectly. By following them in humble and unquestioning obedience, we were led to something quite out of the ordinary.

Ronan was an inveterate quoter. Compulsorily cut off from the common run of humanity, books to him were almost an occupational hazard.

"*Qu'il soit dans le zéphyr qui frémit et qui passe. . . . C'est moi, qui ai vécu,* not a bloody *être factice.*"

"You ought to think up something for yourself now and again," I replied lazily. "Incidentally, you sound like a Frenchman."

"And I speak German like a German, and English like a Scot, *Herzallerliebste mein.*"

"You mimic appallingly well too," I frowned.

"It's why I'm still here. A useful gift in a tight corner. I inherit it from an actor-grandfather . . . character parts. He married a Swiss, an early lady Alpinist. I used to be parked on them, when my father was ill, and I learned very young not to know what I spoke till I listened. It comes back when I want it."

"I see. Do you go to France . . . *now?*"

"Germany mostly," he seemed to think the reply normal.

"I suppose we shouldn't talk like this?"

"I sometimes think I was born for speciality, so help me! My grave was earmarked from my cradle. My other grandfather won the V.C. Genes galore. Not that it affects my appetite. It must be about time to eat."

I collected what little I ever knew of his background in such asides. We were fonder of the specious present. The future meant nothing; the past, for Ronan, at least, was equally taboo.

"We're playing a game," he'd say, "and games have rules. Half-measures are untidy. And sentimental. I don't like the past; it's my future."

"Yet I want to know so much about you."

"Play fair. Do I cross-examine you? Or you encourage it?"

For I, too, insulated myself, and he preferred it so. He didn't even know my married name. I don't think it was caution; I didn't want to use it. As for the rest:

"Everyone calls me Mitty."

"I'm not everyone."

"Marietta then?"

"No; that's too *op*eretta. Just Mari . . . *Mhairi*. Let's be Gaelic! And then I can pretend you belong only to me; forget there's nothing I can do about this whole damned business."

By singling out such conversations, I am distorting the picture. They were rare punctuation marks to our habitual happiness. Ronan was an articulate lover with a gift for translation, and his passionate, poignant delight in the world around him was infectious. We came together; we made an alloy, fused by fire, which was wonderfully durable. We could progress through friendly, pedestrian companionship to high-flown wooing, through blazing physical communion and its afterglow of calm, only to drift round again to tenderness and affection.

"You're my rest," he'd say, "and my longing and my peace." He could talk like that, and seem conversational rather than poetic. "Your eyes are like peat-water reflecting the stars. Most beautiful to me, but then, I'm prejudiced."

The days passed—and the nights.

If I ever hear a siren, even now, twenty years later, he's with me again. I used to pray for a direct hit, so we could go out together, his cheek eternally against mine. I told him. By that time, we could say anything to each other.

"Don't be so daft, love. One of us is enough to placate the gods. You stay alive and like it. As for me, I'd like to die usefully."

I couldn't always avoid the horror of reality. "Are you sure about yourself? Dead sure?"

"An accurate way of putting it. Get it into your head, I haven't a hope. Nor want one. To survive would be to fail, and I don't hold with that. I volunteered. I knew the price. I have the temperament, and the qualifications; I've no one left at all, except Gavin, and he, poor bastard, may well join me inadvertently. No, I'm quite happy about this. Whatever people say, these raids are child's play, and it's my privilege to help them stay that way. It's a good cause, and I'm the man to serve it. That's all."

It is impossible, of course, to describe the fortnight, and

only the general substance is important. This was love sketched on a square of ivory, more readily understood than a diffused canvas, yet none the less beautiful for being in miniature.

"I suppose bored, humdrum people might envy us," I once said.

"Why not." He kissed me lightly. "It's an upside-down world!"

While we stayed in London he was always master of the situation, but one weekend we went down into the country and stayed at an inn crouching among the South Downs. It was not a success. We forgot that moods change with environment. "Captain and Mrs. Grant" on the register embarrassed us. Ronan was anguished that the name was not mine. As one of those rites and gestures all lovers understand he threw away my wedding ring and bought me another, and the pendant, demure pointed diamonds.

As long as we stayed at Mellerton Parva we were subdued, almost domesticated, and I learned a little more in those few days about Ronan. He had been born, he said, where a three-thousand foot top was called a hill and the mountains were Alps and Andes. His passion for climbing had started in Wester Ross as soon as he could walk. He had it still. "Up to the peak, and when you've conquered you feel like a humbled king."

Back in London, the leaves were made of gold. We became wildly gay as a cover for desperation. I used to stare at Ronan, moving from detail to detail; the line of his hair, the well-bred, aquiline nose, that trick he had, now handed down to Mike, of pulling his eyebrows together. . . .

Then suddenly it was all over. Another telephone call from Jock McKechnie. Ronan looked at me sideways but said nothing immediately. First, he crossed the room, and for the thousandth time, adjusted his wretched clock.

"Must you?" I asked sharply.

"It loses too. Would you like it for a souvenir?" His smile was difficult now.

"Certainly not."

We didn't touch each other. It was suddenly forbidden.

"There was a frost this morning," I added irrelevantly.

"How nature does anticipate!" He laughed but his eyes were somber. "My poor autumnal love, next time I'll meet you in spring. So much warmer. I'm sorry, Mari, my very dearest. I have to go at once. Better, I suppose, this way."

"Yes," I agreed.

"But before I leave . . . just this . . . no one was ever more rich and content than I have been with you. If it had been given to love you longer, I couldn't have loved you more."

"We'll meet again," I said. "I feel it."

I saw him off to some uncharted place. I hate railway stations even now. He was of those people who can lend a uniform distinction. Was it the last time he ever wore it?

My face was cupped in his long, blunt fingers. "Cry like hell after I've gone. Get it over, love; well in advance. Don't mourn me, ever, for God's sake. I'm going empty-handed. All my value is left with you."

"I'll keep it safely."

"I'd rather my job than yours. I hope it isn't hell for you. Mari, this is goodbye. Let's not say it. Let's not believe it. My very dear one, my little own one! God help us!"

I went back to tidy up the flat. Ronan Grant had moved forward into his shadowy, menacing world.

I must return to mine.

CHAPTER 9

Aunt Anglesey sat motionless, concentrated, rigid. She was staring at me bewildered, her mouth drooping at corners.

"There you are, Virgil," I said bitterly. "You can let go of my hand. Inferno and purgatory safely traversed. But no paradise. And the wood is just as dark as ever," I added.

"But Mitty . . . !"

"No more. The story's over. Ronan died. It was as if I died with him. Two loves, Ronan and Geoffrey, both lost. I never wanted more. The children are enough, and the memory of vast riches."

"Michael's father!" She spoke absently with the curious shorthand of inner thought. "Truth at the bottom of the well. And it's muddy."

"Do you dare criticize me? Are you trotting out moralities? The smooth ethics of peace for the chaos of war? You know what it was like. That letter! *Eyewitness reports now to hand . . . sufficient time has elapsed . . . a very gallant officer.* Maybe the baby was his. I didn't care. He survives, only in my memory, as I promised him."

She rose abruptly and poured herself a stiff drink.

"Are you celebrating the last of Sigmund Freud?"

"Here's one for you too. Drink it down, child. I'll not be taking up psychiatry after all. I'm only a silly old woman in my dotage, vain of dubious wisdom. I'll know better next time. But how . . . *how* could I have foreseen this? Ronan Grant!"

76

"You sound as if you knew the name."

"Yes," she replied briefly.

"Yet I gave him your address. He didn't know you."

She shook her head. She gulped the rest of her drink.

"He wouldn't then," she said.

"You mean you knew him later?" I was puzzled.

"It's fantastic! It's ridiculous! So are you. You talk of one of the most ruthless, glorious technicolour figures in a stranger-than-fiction war. A man, they say, who may well have saved London from a fate worse than Hiroshima. Sabotage seems to have been his habit. German research installations, a young girl's life, all part of the game."

"You forget I was a very willing victim."

"I should rejoice, perhaps, that a niece of mine should make so interesting a contribution to National Service. Dear Heaven! It's like throwing a jug of cold water over a serenading minstrel! Yet I must do it—Ronan Grant is alive."

"I don't believe it."

"There's always danger in ignorance, child, or believe me, I'd have ducked my duty. I'm not mistaken. I've tried to find any loophole for doubt; I can't. He was eventually Major Grant, Ronan James. The age is right, so is the war record. Everything tallies. He lives in Sussex. He's one of my clients. How's the cold water, my poor lamb?"

It was trickling icily down my spine. I shivered. Miracles in everyday life are oddly repulsive. Lazarus must have been something of an embarrassment to his friends.

"He would have let me know," I protested.

"O Mitty child! How can I disenchant you? It's not so much that your lover is alive; you have to learn he never existed. He's a fantasy. You played a child's game. It's over now."

"Very well. So he's alive. Mike loses all dignity of conception. I was a traitor for nothing. Most sins, I suppose, are sired by stupidity."

"Don't look so lost, child. They are also absolved by honesty."

"I presume I'm not having a nightmare."

"You need facts for the new image. Mr. R. Grant of The Grange, Stoke Hempstead. Middle-aged, in poor health, bad-tempered, and hard to please. He is a gentleman with an exaggerated idea of his own value, I fancy, though financially at least that's pretty high. He spends more on a new car than you on all his son's upbringing. In the City, I imagine he often turns over more in a day than would keep you for life. He's a widower. The wife died a few years back of an overdose of barbiturates. The marriage was childless and was said to be unhappy, sympathy being mostly with the woman. It now looks as if that Linley-Morgan chit is to step into Faith Grant's shoes. A very decorative young person, not much older than Renata, but presumably prepared, like her mother before her, to do anything for money."

"The more you tell me, the less I can believe."

"He's to the forefront of my mind just now, ironically enough. He wants a new secretary-housekeeper and he's the very devil to suit. I've sent him fifteen to date, all possible. Yet now he has the impertinence to advertise in *The Times*."

It was strange how that piece of information brought me at last to reality. Up till then, I had listened as though to an absorbing work of fiction whose spell would evaporate once the book were closed. Now my eyes slid furtively toward the bedside table where I could see my mark in the Personal Column. It was a job which had sounded attractive. Its requirements were well within my scope; the conditions ideal, if, as they all suggested, I let the Pargiton house with a view to selling later. The very name, R. Grant, unlikely as it was, had seemed a good omen. I had been thinking about it seriously.

The narrowness of my escape jolted me. If, unwittingly, I had suddenly found myself face to face with Ronan Grant! The thought was shattering. For the first time, I was truly grateful to my aunt, and my muddled resentment dropped away.

"When did you meet him first?" I asked more naturally.

She was so hesitant, I had to smile. "Come on," I said. "Fair's fair. I've told you everything; far too much as it turns out. Any information gratefully accepted. It could help with Michael who's so like him."

"Do you think so? I don't see it myself. It wasn't as if he were so very old when I first ran across him. I suppose his fragility was misleading. He had no more substance than thistledown, and Mike is such a husky boy."

"That doesn't sound like Ronan. He was slighter than Michael perhaps, but very tough."

Again she hesitated. "It was after the war, child. You saw what it did to others. He wasn't exempt. He'd paid in rough coin. Originally, he came to me for a job. I wish I could remember the date; perhaps Lavinia Wolstencroft can place it. She had a soft spot for the boy. She likes them dark and delicate. It was in the days of warrior resettlement, and what a sober hobby it was! We were torn between waning patriotism, active pity, and solid business requirements. Young Grant eptiomized my problem. He was a haughty young man, tense almost to breaking-point, ill enough to be unreliable, and in addition, abrupt, even rude in manner. Yet, though he didn't look fit to be out of his bed, he curled up at any reference to his plight. I didn't like him, and I'll tell you why. Curious, I should only now find a possible explanation for what puzzled me so much at the time. He opened our interview with a cock-and-bull story which smacked

79

of the confidence trick. I realize now it was a clumsy way of inquiring about you, but I can only say he made it sound glib. He was at home, I suppose, with a lie for a cover story. I gave him a pretty sharp reply, though now I see I told him everything he wanted to know."

"Which was?"

"That you had a husband and three infants and were perfectly happy."

"I see."

"Don't blame me. I spoke the truth as I knew it, and it was all so phrased, his inquiry, that it could well have been a crutch to get him a job. He pretended he'd served with your son, whose father had been killed in the Blitz. I merely corrected his error. But in fact, I did get him a job with some profiteers who never kept their staff anyway. And I was surprised that young Grant accepted it, so surprised I thought I'd better keep an eye on him. He didn't last long. He was back in hospital within a fortnight with a serious relapse."

"Lavinia kept fussing. As I say, she had a *tendre* for him, and in the end, to keep her quiet, I telephoned the military authority concerned. They were rather vague about Major Grant's condition, but interested in me. Would I like to see him? He had no visitors. He seemed very much alone. It was one of those charities you regret immediately, but there's a lot to be said for giving free entertainment, so I put on my most outrageous garments, and set off with a bunch of grapes."

"My progress through the general ward was a huge success, and they enjoyed my nineteen-fourteen repartee. Young Grant, however, was in a private room. He lay looking like his own effigy in wax. His appearance shocked me. I even wondered momentarily if he could be alive. Obviously, the boy was in no state to receive a stranger. Yet they'd asked me to try and rouse him for he took no interest in anything."

"For a long time, I sat beside him, feeling the worst sort of impostor. After all, I hardly knew him, and hadn't liked him, poor lad. You know how it is; continuing silence puts odd thoughts in your head which should never be there. My mind took a strange turn. You didn't know perhaps, I lost a baby when Tom died. About the same age, I thought; women are basically sentimental. I gave way to an impulse, taking his hand in mine. It was a poor thing, bitterly thin, every muscle and tendon showing beneath the papery skin. And then he opened his eyes for the first time and stared at me with an expression which was impossible to read.

"The baroque Mrs. Anglesey!" he murmured, and promptly withdrew his hand. I was vaguely surprised he could make such a deliberate movement. Hurt too.

"I thought I'd look in on you and see how you progressed," I said hastily to cover my embarrassment.

"I don't."

"You will." But I was by no means sure.

"Why should you care one way or the other?"

"My dear boy," I snapped. "I don't. I'm merely trying to make conversation. By order I may say."

"Admirable choice." He spoke throughout very econom-ically with long pauses beteeen words, which he dragged and slurred.

"They labour under the delusion I'm a relative, which, I thank heaven, is not the case. My kith and kin are mildly exasperating, but you exceed them. Have you anyone of your own?"

"No more. My brother was killed."

"So obviously you need a rousing aunt."

"Related to your matronly niece?"

I looked at him sharply. He mocked without humour.

"Why did you produce that very thin story?" I asked curiously. He didn't look at me very often. Mostly he stared at the ceiling.

"Line-shooting . . . sales-talk. . . ."

"Truth would have been better."

His short laugh ended in a cough which seemed to cause him considerable pain. His features sharpened and he closed his eyes again. I could escape.

But I looked back. He was staring at me with weary speculation.

"Enough duty for one day?" he asked.

"Would you like me to come again?"

He shook his head. "My period of hope is over," he said.

"Nonsense! Before I go, you must promise to come and see me as soon as you're better. I'm serious."

"Very well." You could see he was humouring me, and for the first time, there was possibly an undertone of amusement. "I'd like to chauffeur a Bentley by the way."

"Good! I'll find you one." It was much more likely I'd read his obituary in *The Times*, I thought.

He knew it. His eyes quizzed me. He nearly achieved a facial expression.

"How surprised you'd be! Goodbye, Mrs. Anglesey. No flowers by request. And give my love to your so-domesticated niece."

My anger was sluggish, dull, misleading as referred pain. For some reason, it focussed irrelevantly on my poor aunt, who, betraying a rare tenderness, had been spurned and never forgotten it. Nor was there excuse for mocking that unfortunate niece, even then.

"What was the trouble?" I asked.

"I had no sooner left him than his doctor buttonholed me.

"At least he talked to you," he pointed out. "He's virtually dumb with us. Surgically, even medically, we make head-way. Psychologically we draw a blank every time."

"What we used to call shell-shock, I suppose."

"Not really. That implies something more immediate. At last we've managed to get in touch with the German surgeon who sorted him out at the time. What was interesting was his liking for the boy, whom he found cooperative, amusing, and very responsible about the morale of his fellow unfortunates. But now he's getting worse and worse, and showing no fight at all. Couldn't care less, as they say. I wish I knew more about him."

"I'm afraid we have only the most superficial acquaintance. I don't even know an outline of his history."

"And I only his war record, which is startling. One can only give a summary. The security people are still very strict. But you've probably heard of the Meisterhafen raid. It was a suicide assignment, but the Gestapo ironically saved his life. What with one thing and another, they never expected anyone in that condition to escape, but they reckoned without Ronan Grant, who not only managed to make his way out of Germany, but neglected and ill though he was, organized a most complicated network of underground resistance. Unfortunately, after the first patching up, there was very little medical attention about all this, and it's late to start now. We do our best, but not what is necessary."

I never expected to see young Major Grant again.

It must have been over a year later when he walked into my office. He was leaning on a stick, but he looked better —and much older. He had acquired a habit of twisting his mouth slightly to keep pain in order. It suited his manner.

"Good afternoon, Mrs. Anglesey. You did invite me to come. So here I am. I felt I should call and thank you for reminding me I don't die easily."

"Did I?"

"You wore a 'farewell forever' look—a thing I detest. It annoyed me and I decided to prove you wrong. An amusing reason for continued and pointless existence, but all in a piece with the rest of the game. I'm not in the least grateful —that is spared you. Nor do I want one of your jobs. I already supplement a total disability pension by pen-pushing for a philanthropic old gentleman who must have been deprived of the Boys' Own Paper in impressionable early childhood. Nothing is too bloodthirsty to spoil the flavour of the tea and coffee we drink together. I'm a walking Christmas Number. The handicapped hero finds his level. Extraordinary!"

He spoke rather fast and too fluently.

"You must give yourself time, and there are other jobs meanwhile."

"But chiefly domestic, aren't they? My wife would consider them *déclassé*. She's a snob."

"You're married?"

"Surprising, isn't it?" he went on in his new voice. "You'd wonder anyone would take me on. But my dear Mrs. Anglesey, it is a sad and sober truth that any wreck can get married. I'm living proof of it. The fact is if you haunt hospitals long enough, there's always one nurse so desperate for a husband, she jibs at no one. How convenient that is! The meths and talc expert always to hand; the hypodermic everlastingly poised at the ready."

"So it seems!" I countered tartly.

He went rather quickly.

Another year passed, and this time it was Mrs. Grant who paid us a visit. She was a heavy young woman, mink-swathed and far too lavishly made-up. You know those jokes about nurses out of uniform; she was the type who had originated them. Then too, she had the grand, executive manner of a ward sister, self-satisfied and condescending.

To my surprise, she required a chauffeur, a careful driver with experience of Rolls-Royces and Bentleys. No other duties. There were two gardeners always, and her husband kept a valet. You can imagine we hastily tapped our grapevine and learned that an obscure Grant of venerable years had dropped a large fortune into the lap of an unknown collateral, choosing the one with the best war record, for want of any better reason. Young Grant took over his new empire with interest, immediately showing toughness, shrewdness, and even a trace of financial genius. He had something to keep his mind occupied.

He settled down to be miserable in comfort. His health was still very poor and his temper worse, according to the bridge table acquaintances of his wife. A divorce, indeed, would have surprised no one. When she died, rumours circulated freely. Luckily for him, it turned out she had a weak heart. The verdict was accidental death, and that was that.

"So Mitty, that's all I can tell you. He uses the Agency, of course, but I seldom see him myself. The last time was at a party, quite recently, when, I may say, he deliberately avoided me. He was flanked by Linley-Morgans, seemingly very taken with the girl, who was eager and vivacious as a James Thurber drawing. They say the mother tried first without much success. I've heard he wants an heir, and I identified his assessing look, as that of a shrewd stockman in a cattle market. He's a man who wants value for money. Not your country, Mitty."

"I'll digest this all gradually, I suppose."

"Poor child! You must want to wring my neck. But you'll end by thanking me. Women cling so grimly to their illusions. If yours helped you through bad days—good! But it's now time to throw them out the window. You're young enough to break free and build your life on firmer foundations."

"You must be tired, Aunt Trix, to sound so pleading! Why don't you go to bed? I've had enough too."

"You'll be all right? You'll sleep?"

"Oddly enough—yes."

Her goodnight was almost embarrassingly affectionate. Fond as I was of her, I didn't want her pity.

The risen Ronan. I accepted him now. Come to think it, there'd always been a life-sized solidity about his ghost. As if he were nearer than I thought . . . encroaching on me— but you dream strange dreams when you're lonely.

I was dry-eyed, tired.

The stars were setting, another day would come.

Cadenza

CHAPTER 10

Morning came and with it spring.

The sun shone; the London plane trees were alert.

I looked out of the window. I breathed deeply.

I was out of mourning for a twenty-year-old war.

There was a curious lightness in me. Ronan was alive. As I was alive, quickening to a new world.

Now I was free. Free! Yet glad he was on the same earth.

My one love, my young love—old like me!

The long mirror was suddenly reflecting a stranger. If Ronan were myth, what had happened to the girl who had created it. "What pretty curls!" "I think you're most beautiful." He should see me now! Mrs. Brandon, mother of three. She was nothing to do with young Mitty Peters.

He wouldn't recognize me. He could fall over me and never know who I was. How drab and limp with my scraped hair and dowdy suit. He'd probably forgotten my existence.

All right; I wanted to see him. I wanted to look at him, count his wrinkles, ask myself how I had come to be so mistaken, hate him for it, and start again. To nullify the spell required his presence. I didn't want to dismiss the lover and be haunted by a pale effigy staring at a hospital ceiling. Ought I to be grateful that he'd spared me that final problem, when I could only just cope, as it was? For I'd have gone to him—of course I would! No use pretending otherwise.

Perhaps I should have known; known he'd wanted me, needed me. Nonsense! I'd never pretended to second-sight.

Since my illness my clothes were far too big for me. I'd once had a nice figure and worn a suit elegantly. I needed a hairdresser these days; I was a Brontë travesty. In an unfashionable hat and my National Health reading spectacles— could there be anything more hideous? All that was required to complete the picture was a copy of yesterday's *Times*.

Aunt Anglesey was busy in her office; George recommended walking in the sunshine; wasn't Green's Hotel just round the corner? It was so easy . . . so *easy!* Pick up the phone; make an appointment; for the same afternoon. Mr. Grant would see me. I should see him too. Once only. And for the last time.

Part Two

CHAPTER 11

The man rose to greet me belatedly.

"Now you'll be Mrs. Brandon," he said.

A stoop subtracted from his real height, though this was reemphasized by skeletal meagerness. His expression was bored and restricted, the crows'-feet round his eyes indicating irritation rather than good-humour. In such a thin face, the neat, arrogant nose, the stubborn jawline were highlighted. His subdued hair was neutralized by a fine dusting of silver. Where was the vivid boy from the past? This was a stranger.

"Do please sit down."

I obeyed his orders and faced him across the desk. He adjusted heavy, horn-rimmed spectacles better to study my papers. They threw his uncompromising pallor into relief and screened him. All power of comparison slithered away. It was easier to look at the new man with new eyes.

"An unusual sort of applicant," he commented. I was to learn he alternated between the curt statement and a tired drawl. What had he done with his pretty brogue? If you imitated the Southron too long, it became second nature.

Absurd I should have worshipped and agonized all these years. Why had I come? I was shattering the spell too quickly and efficiently.

"I doubt if I'm what you need," I answered coolly. The situation was comfortably safe with fifteen predecessors rejected.

"That's for me to decide, Mrs. Brandon."

I didn't like his tone. Nor him. It was time for my rehearsed speech.

"I happened to see your advertisement in *The Times*. I needed a job badly, though I know I'm not really the type." In my experience, a slight air of desperation seldom recommends and I was determined to disobey all rules on how to gain friends and influence people. I next decided he looked so fragile, it was safe to assume he'd dislike the symptoms of others.

"I've been ill, you see," I added and settled down to spare him nothing.

"And you're better now?" he sounded, as I ended, most suitably bored.

"I haven't tried working yet. That's why I thought of this job. I doubt if I could stand up to London Transport twice a day. Or even London."

"You're a shorthand-typist?"

"Very out of practice. I daresay it would come back."

"And can drive a car?"

"I'm not good in traffic." This was a half-truth; the boys said an astronaut lived less dangerously than my passengers round Hyde Park Corner.

I suppose the other applicants had been more enthusiastic. He took off his glasses, and for the first time studied me speculatively. He didn't recognize me; I was certain of that. This was the glance of an entomologist selecting a crawling creature from an insectarium. I looked away. His eyes were still dark as wet slate, a colour I knew in the days I walked up to *Creag Dubh* from the croft, when the rain swept across the hills of his homeland, and the wind played around the corries.

"I live in the country," he was explaining quietly. "The traffic is not immoderate. It's a question of mobility. I only keep one chauffeur and need him myself."

I was tempted to resort to sarcasm. It seemed so odd to have a chauffeur at all. As for *more* than one!

"I'm not used to a big house," I tried hopefully.

"Mine runs itself. An excellent staff, who know my ways. No difficulty about that."

"I wonder you need a housekeeper."

"The women are foreigners, and I'm often away. I prefer to leave a native in charge. As for the secretarial work, it's within anyone's scope. The worst of it goes to my City office, but I like to have someone on hand when I'm ill. Like you, I find travelling exhausting."

I saw no parallel. What had Mr. Grant, chauffeur-driven to complain of? Think of all the other war casualties straphanging through middle age, and weary women shuffling through three jobs at once. He was beginning to annoy me; I'd vote Left at the next Election; damned plutocrat! And Michael needing a new suit!

I controlled myself. The game wasn't going according to plan. I had not been so clever after all. Michael! Too late, I remembered such males enjoyed an obstacle race. They decided their course of action well in advance and pursued it undeflected by difficulty or opposition. Well, do did I.

"The money isn't really enough," a new avenue of escape, and a cruder one.

"How about your previous salary—all found?"

"But . . . !" I gasped. "But that's ridiculous! I was quite senior. It's far too much!"

"Allow me to be the judge of that. Money is the least of my concerns. And I think you'd do."

Anger is a poor counsellor, and suddenly it really warmed me. I'd done my best. This was the result. It didn't matter much what I said now. I abandoned my prepared manifesto as happily as a post-election politician. Damn Ronan Grant, his money and his job!

"I should explain," I improvized. "I plan to deceive you. I'm a widow with a young family and have no intention of leaving them for more than a period of convalescence. And because I can't afford a country holiday, I must work my way. Unfortunately, temporary jobs seem nonexistent at the moment. *I thought you'd do!*"

He took my riposte without a trace of expression.

"We could fix a week's notice then, on either side. My own requirements might well change in the near future. And, after all, you may not suit me."

"That, I should have thought, was self-evident."

"Or I might not suit you."

"Obviously."

"Oh come now, Mrs. Brandon." He kept his poker-face but his voice hid amusement. It added fuel to my fire.

"I don't want your job."

"So I see. Yet it's so suitable. You have such complex requirements, such modest attainments. You say you need the money. Oughtn't you to swallow your temperament and your particularity about employers?"

"I'm sure you've plenty of alternatives."

"Yes, indeed. But between ourselves they all promise to be *devoted,* and what is more tedious? Now you seem quite determined to dislike me. I find that admirable."

It would have given me great pleasure to slap him. Either he was teasing me, or his vanity was completely out of hand. Either explanation was exasperating.

"In other words, you woke up this morning and decided to fill your vacancy before nightfall. Typical!" Annoyance was outweighing discretion.

"Could be." He spoke softly. "How did you know?"

"Just the sort of thing you would do!"

"So? You're a student of character, Mrs. Brandon?"

"I've worked with people for ten years. Successfully."

"Then you should know better than to be afraid of me."

"Afraid of you, Mr. Grant? You flatter yourself. I dislike being pushed into position, that's all. It's true, you offer me an ideal job for my present circumstances. I'm more than equal to it, too. Particularly your final requirement. I don't dote under optimum conditions."

He shrugged. "I'm bad-tempered, and so are you. We might achieve armed neutrality. So restful."

To this day, I don't know how it happened. Presumably I was punch-drunk by that time, lost in a labyrinth of conflicting emotions, all of them unpleasant. Historically, I was silly about *dares*, and this challenge lay in front of me like a gauntlet. I would far rather prove that I paused to contemplate my nonexistent bank balance, or wished to catch a closer view of the extraordinary nature which had prompted Michael's. I'd admit to feminine submissiveness, sheer exhaustion, but it wouldn't be honest. All I can remember is the anger, the warm, vital anger which soothed and replaced, not only the dull ache of disenchantment, but also the sharp pain of humiliation.

If he had recognized me . . . but he wouldn't now. I didn't recognize myself.

"When would you want me?" I asked coldly.

That agreement was ratified without further altercation was due to destiny taking a hand. I had no sooner finished speaking, when a girl entered the room. So this was Carolyn Linley Morgan! Very decorative certainly, artists' material rather than the stuff of cheap prettiness. A small, gamin face, a sleek dark head, wide-flecked hazel eyes, oddly like my own. I was aware of astuteness, and perhaps sensibility, but she used a world-weary languor, ill-suited to her years.

"Ronnie darling, you owe me an apology," she began without preamble. "I've come to claim it—and some tea. You didn't miss a thing. But you might have let me know earlier, so I could have got out of it too."

"I'm duly contrite, Carolyn, but I've been working non-stop for two days."

"Poor Ronnie! Yes, you do look exhausted. And who's this?"

"This is Mrs. Brandon. She's just agreed to come to the Grange." I hadn't really reached that point, but didn't feel like arguing at that particular moment. She was looking me up and down with ill-concealed amusement and noting my faded drabness with scorn and satisfaction.

"Well, that's a relief. We can relax. I was afraid you'd have to recall old Wilk from exile. And she'd come—at the double!"

That quick contraction of eyebrows! Michael's scowl. Miss Linley-Morgan was not immune from Mr. Grant's displeasure. I, too, had a final confirmation of what still seemed incredible. She was welcome to him!

"Then we'll meet again," she dismissed me with mild courtesy and no enthusiasm. "Ronnie, are you taking me out to dinner tonight?"

"I really must get back to Stoke Hempstead. You're lucky to get tea. You'll join us, Mrs. Brandon, I hope."

"I really must be going."

"Are you sure? Then we must settle a date. . . ."

In the street, I emerged from a trance, and knew I had bought myself a front-row seat on the edge of a volcano. Of all the damned silly things! I was frightened by my own stupidity. I could produce wonderful arguments in favour of this scheme, but they were nullified by one uncomfortable truth. I had been moved like a pawn—and by Ronan Grant!

Who cared? Simpler to ignore it. The last twenty-four hours had been so emotional, the whole thing was beginning to bore me. Anyhow, for the sum of threepence, I could send Mr. Grant packing. At least you can't be hypnotized by post. Yet hardly worth it. There'd still been protest in me when that girl joined us. It was she who had subtly altered the situation. With a lovely young creature like that at his disposal, the appalling Mr. Grant was unlikely to worry about Mrs. Brandon—or his past. He had a future.

I was still mulling these matters over in my mind as I sat that evening in coward silence, listening to my aunt's bracing conversation. Preoccupied with my renaissance, she was recommending everything from Nureyev to face-lifters. Life, she told me, could still hold infinite possibility and pleasure. It was merely a question of training the palate to appreciate subtler flavours.

"Yes," I agreed meekly. She had insisted I too should struggle with needlework. It was a useful trick. I could bend my head over it and hide my face.

"Now we've cleared the decks, you must allow yourself to develop. Become a person in your own right before the children leave you high and dry. And remember, they most certainly will."

"Yes," I said again.

"It's time you left Pargiton . . . such a dismal place . . . Geoffrey wants to share this flat in London with his friend; Mike's home less and less; as for Ren, Lucy is quite right when she says it's no background for an emerging girl. You have this offer for the house, Mitty. Take it."

"They want it furnished first, I believe. That would suit me better."

"Good! It's a start. You won't return, and you'll go on holiday all the sooner."

"On holiday?"

"North Africa is very pleasant at this time of year. I'll pay. And when you return, Mitty, like a giant refreshed, we'll talk business. It's time you came into partnership with me."

"But Aunt Trix," I gasped incredulously.

"No *buts*. It's the obvious thing. I'm not as young as I was. This Agency's hard work. But we have a small gold mine at our disposal, if we move with the day and age. The trouble is to find a replacement personality. My own style is inimitable, and besides it would be a bore to reduplicate it. Now 'Mrs. Brandon,' I see exactly. Of well-bred appearance, gentle and sympathetic, favouring mauves and lilac greys."

"With my colouring?"

"You'll dye your hair blue," she replied cheerfully.

It was funny, yes; but I didn't laugh.

"I know, Aunt Trix, you mean well . . ." I began.

"Don't interrupt, child! Naturally, we must work things out gradually, but I intend you to inherit my kingdom when I go. You're the heiress I'd choose. Whoever takes over and perpetuates my name, gets this property and the bulk of the capital as well."

How very odd, I should suddenly find myself actually grateful to Mr. Grant, who had so inadvertently extricated me from a fate worse than death. To work in double-harness with my astringent aunt would surely reduce me to pummelled submission. If it were my lot to be pushed and crushed, let it be with one week's notice on either side!

"There's something I must tell you," I said more authoritatively. "I do appreciate your very kind and flattering offer, but I must refuse, little as I enjoy doing so. I can think of many reasons, but it's easier to give one. I'm not free. Even to take a holiday. You can cross the Grant vacancy off your books."

"*What?*"

It was my turn to press on defiantly.

"I applied for the job—a spurious interview being a way of taking a look at him. I had to, you know. Get him moved forward in time. That was all right. He didn't recognize me, and frankly I shouldn't have known him. The trouble was he offered me the job. You realize yourself what an admirable stop-gap it would be—with any other employer—especially as he's now in favour of a temporary appointment. A safe berth so I can let my house; no daily travel; no housework. Use of a car; settled staff; excellent salary; no strings. And what an opportunity to find out what prompts Mike's awkward, aggressive nature. I agree with you Mr. Grant is rather insufferable. One suspects this is a most efficient way of inoculating myself against future attacks of Ronanitis. The children are all busy and out of the way. And, incidentally, I'm broke."

"You protest too much, Mitty. Of all the idiotic things! If you have any sense at all, which sometimes I doubt, you'll write at once and put him off. Better still, I'll do it for you."

"Oh no! For I plunged straight into *The Times* advertisement. The name of Anglesey might alert him."

"I suppose you're still besotted."

"My dear aunt." My drawl was something like Ronan's. "I'd have preferred to have kept him in grave clothes, but it wasn't allowed. Incidentally I met the Linley-Morgan girl too. Not a bad girl. I felt rather sorry for her."

"You needn't waste sympathy on Linley-Morgans. They know what they're doing. Up to the ears in debt, I should think, and no illusions. Elvira knew Faith Grant well, and won't expect an ideal domestic pet. As for Carolyn, she's a divorce-child; they often like them elderly. Personally I think her a spoiled, ill-mannered little minx."

"It all sounds most appropriate."

"But it's you, child, I'm worried about. What happens if he recognizes you?"

"I've thought of that, of course. Does it matter? I can always say: 'Didn't we meet during the War? But how interesting!'"

She smiled grimly. "I'd like to hear it—if, and only if, there were no Michael. True, he's a by-product, but remember Grant has no children."

"Mike never comes within a mile during term. A meeting's practically impossible."

She decided, I think, that argument was only likely to bake the clay. I have an obstinate reputation. Next day, she merely presented me with the Grant dossier. It made interesting reading, and I was glad to get my situation in three dimensions. Two French maids. Daily help. Eight principal bedrooms. From there, I firmly recalled the despair, the confusion with which I had recently faced unemployment. I could now return to Pargiton, far better circumstanced, and less worried, than in that emotional limbo I had found in Mayfair.

The illusion was fostered by Geoffrey, who dispersed any feeling of strangeness. He had piled the fire halfway up the chimney, and now poured me a South African sherry.

"Drink to the remittance of your sentence, Mum," he recommended. "Or are you only out on parole?"

"I prefer Colonial Pale to fine old Manzanilla," I sighed comfortably. "It's good to be home. I feel as if I've been run over by a Juggernaut."

"I expect you have! Poor old Mum! But how could we

rescue you? You were really ill, and we very neglectful. With the choice between great-aunt and Gran . . . well! See what I mean?"

"You've had it too, I hear. Well, G., you'll soon be in London and can do what you please."

"Helga? Haven't you noticed my carefree appearance? They saved me the bother of getting rid of her myself."

"Some people are cool!"

"I shall now devote my life to my Mum," he retaliated. "Not that I'll get much chance if you bury yourself in Sussex. Besides, I shall be working too hard to fulfil my duties. Imagine that. I've decided to turn over a new leaf."

"Not before time," I retorted.

You never knew when Geoffrey was serious. Perhaps he meant it. Certainly he was my prop through the next week. I found myself actually leaning on him, and he was very anxious to be companionable. Mike and Ren sent me innumerable postcards full of specific instructions, but it was Geoffrey who carried them out. This display of conscience alerted my own.

"I ought to tell you," I said one night, "that my stay in Falloden Street had a strange sequel. Aunt Trix asked me to go into partnership with her."

"Actually Gran's always said that's the answer."

"This was take it or leave it. I left it. But I think she'll strike again, and if I continue to refuse, we can say goodbye to inheritance. The Brandons will be out."

"Blackmail, eh? Old so-and-so! Softens you up, and names the price."

"She meant well, G. Security for us all. She's fond of us. I suppose I ought to have accepted eagerly. But she's such an Earth-Shaker! Even a fortnight of her normal company is overpowering. I just can't see myself her eternal stooge. Anyhow, that's the position. What do you think?"

"I'm glad you refused."

"Yet it doesn't affect you quite as much as the others. It would have given you all a better start."

"We've been starting for years." He grinned. "Time we stopped for a change. Don't be a jellyfish, Mum. We've always managed somehow."

"With much-needed help from Aunt Anglesey," I pointed out.

"Well, Hell's Bells! I'd respect her more if she didn't remind us of it. Surely it's one of the Great Rights—to make a mess of your own life in your own way. If it's not in the Atlantic Charter, it ought to be. Who wants to live successfully to someone else's blueprint?"

"All right. Let's go to the devil in our own way."

"That's my Mum," he said.

CHAPTER 12

The Grange, Stoke Hempstead, was set in a pretty district, so varnished by affluence as to appear unreal. Even the hedges and ditches suggested the meticulous landscaper. On a calendar, I would have been charmed; face to face, it all looked self-conscious.

The black Rolls, purring like a cat, turned left between virginal gates and picked its way up a weedless avenue. Velour lawns skirted an old, well-groomed house, whose faultless architecture pleaded for some irrelevant excrescence. On its portico steps, two dogs, their pedigrees engraved in their faces, kept heraldic guard and mournfully raised their aristocratic heads to despise the passerby. The door was opened by a parlourmaid, anachronistic in afternoon uniform. She actually bobbed me a brief, continental curtsey.

"You, Mrs. Brandon. Me, I am Annette." With such simple words, she preceded me into a hall like a film set, her sturdy peasant contours bouncing on high stiletto heels.

"Is Mr. Grant at home?"

"*Mais oui*, Madame. He has his tea but it is nearly finish. You too must have yours. Later, I show you your room, when Pullen, he have brought in your baggages."

"Yes, perhaps that would be best," I murmured, conscious I wanted to plunge in while my nerve was still good.

"Madame . . . Mam'selle Linley-Morgan, they too are here." I make only a superficial attempt to reproduce Annette's accent, which I came to find expressive, and *very* fluent. She was tiny, full of vivacity, and very young.

The drawing room was pure Antique Dealers' Fair from its Aubussoned floor to its dark, Spanish mahogany. The soft furnishings could only be described as sumptuous. The temperature was equatorial; the effect was stifling.

My mother always held that few women could lean back against silk brocade and subtract from it, a signal for my father to point out she was one of them. Natural, perhaps, to think of Mother, who always put an elegant room in its place. This could not be said of the big, blonde woman who presided over a heavy, silver tea tray, while her daughter slumped languidly on a disapproving eighteenth-century sofa. My new employer was leaning against the fireplace—Adam, of course! If I were to be an actress, the stage set was certainly traditional!

"Ah, Mrs. Brandon!" He introduced me courteously to Mrs. Linley-Morgan who rapidly calculated the cost of everything I wore, asked me if I took sugar, and hearing I did not, gave me two lumps.

I melted into invisibility, no problem about it.

When I had eaten three delicious cakes and finished up the cucumber sandwiches, I decided I'd had enough of mouselike anonymity, and made a tactful escape.

Annette was a different proposition. Having shown me my new quarters, she lingered.

"This is the room of Meeswilk," she informed me, and I was always to think of my predecessor by that portmanteau title. "Meeswilk, she was my friend. When I am little, she buy me bonbons and teach me the English. I speak it pretty —yes? Not like my good aunt Simone."

"Have you been in England a long time?"

"*Mais oui,* Madame. It is since many years. You will comprehend, everyone, they die, and there is no money. M'sieur, he come and fetch me, and my Aunt too, to bring us here."

"And your aunt Simone is cook?"

"She is a ver' good cook. Whatever they are saying, Those Ones—she is magnificent. This, I tell you, Madame, one time she was cooking for a proper Duc. But M'sieur he give her more money, and say she must bring me out. And if I am good, and ver' old, he give me the fine *dot,* so I married."

A voluble child, but I was well-conditioned and she made me feel less homesick. I thought better of my employer too for taking care of her. As she spoke, she was deftly unpacking the unimpressive contents of my suitcases, her eyes lighting at the emergence of the Anglesey bedwear.

"O so pretty! You are not at all like Meeswilk who spend much money on dresses and nothing on bedclothes. Simone say that is right. Me, I am like you."

I nearly explained that my "bedclothes" were a gift, but I remembered in time not to give out gratuitous information.

"Aren't you busy," I said hastily, "with visitors in the house? I'm used to unpacking for myself."

"But I enjoy helping, Madame. We will be friends, yes? I will help you much. You need not say like Those Ones: 'Iron this dress, Annette! Here, my keys!' They should bring their own maid, if they have one."

Her tirade was interrupted by a middle-aged woman who sent her scurrying. I was now examined carefully, with no hint as to conclusions, and addressed with extreme formality.

"I hope Madame Brandon is happy here."

Simone had no aitches; the effect was odd!

"How do you do!" I matched her tone. "And is there anything I can do? Any way I can help?"

"All is well. Do not disarrange yourself, Madame. Meeswilk, she leave the house to me in entirety."

I welcomed this broad hint. I was grateful the prevailing domestic efficiency would be no concern of mine. When had I had experience in such perfection? Dinner, when it came, was superbly cooked and served, so I was amazed at the effrontery of Elvira Linley-Morgan, who buttonholed the Frenchwoman and, after a grudging compliment, suggested better recipes for nearly every item.

"Mama knows how to cook the weirdest dishes," Carolyn remarked as we withdrew. "She's fabulous really, for she never goes near a stove."

"A pity, perhaps, to upset someone else's cook," I replied pointedly.

"A few well-chosen words in absolutely incomprehensible *patois* will put that right," she shrugged. "Ronnie just sends them. The sun rises and sets with him . . . their *cher M'sieur!*"

"They're remarkably good servants."

"Too good, Mrs. Brandon. They think they own the place. Actually, they have loads of help. Old Wilk lived like a duchess. Silly idiot! Designs on the boss, of course."

The arrival of her mother and her host put an end to the conversation. I drank coffee out of a Meissen cup, odd contrast to the cracked willow-pattern of Regent's Park, if Regent's Park ever existed. This persistent unreality! I felt I had walked into the second act of an expensive production, understudying Meeswilk to admiration.

"Aren't you eager to get to bed?"

I jumped as Elvira addressed me unexpectedly. I had not yet finished my coffee. She was a bit previous.

"Journeys are so tiring," she added firmly.

I smiled. "I've only come from Pargiton."

"Unpacking too," she persisted.

"Annette very kindly did that for me."

"How extraordinary. She's usually so unhelpful, and of course servants can be so awkward with. . . ." Her voice trailed away as she remembered the date and century. "Do you enjoy secretarial work?" she asked.

I'm afraid I requested more coffee. I had an itch to annoy her. We were natural enemies. A lot of my mother in me, I suppose, but the snobbery had become inverted. Not that I didn't welcome the excuse to escape, but it could have been less clumsily presented. She escorted me upstairs soon after, aggressively lecturing me on the joys of early nights, and my lack of chaperon duties. For myself, I meditated on her shortcomings as a mother. There was much to be said for the old game of an accidental session alone in the conservatory. Such pushing and creaking maneuvres were surely wrong.

Carolyn's hand was still ringless. Presumably no notices in *Times* and *Telegraph* either, to trap the victim finally. Everything suggested I would be in at the kill. I wouldn't enjoy it. Carolyn might be a nice child with a different mother. How could they do it? Were show-houses and City companies adequate compensations for the loss of a hopeful start? Mr. Grant, too, was quite aware of their tactics, which he appeared to regard with a twisted amusement which might well have repercussions at a later date.

Sunday must have been uneventful for I can only recall I went to church twice in one day, wondering if the Linley-Morgans had been introduced into my life so I could prosper spiritually. I decided that if Elvira were a habitual weekender, I would probably finish with a fair imitation of religious mania.

It was Monday before I saw the library—at last a well-used, shabby room! There were numerous, old, untidy books; the sporting prints were miscellaneous; the missing telephone directories and dog-leads lay helter-skelter. It was quite a relief to see the paraphernalia of everyday life again. There were photographs too. The dark woman in white with a tartan sash was very like the young officer in naval uniform, who in turn bore a startling resemblance to my second son. Rather to my surprise, young Ronan, captaining a school Rugby side, or laughing with a group of young subalterns in kilts, was not nearly so familiar. He was a slight boy with his eyes screwed up. It was Gavin Grant's replica whose picture was in my wallet.

Like an agent, taking an inventory, I moved round till I reached the fireplace and found with a real sense of shock, my passport back into the war years. The clock, our clock! Unbombed, unchanged, it was still half-a-minute wrong! It stood on the mantel, friendly and hideous, souvenir of some long-lost Victorian diningroom, and smiled down on me blandly, like an ironic conspirator.

A shameful wave of sentimentality gathered, poised, and

flooded me. I brushed my eyes angrily. How the Hell could he forget? Or look at that damned thing every day? Or hadn't he really believed it was recording his last hours on earth? Had it all been a game?

Embarrassed by myself, I went over to the table and stripped off the typewriter cover. None too soon, for Mr. Grant, his guests safely off the premises, now entered the room, and talked about starting work.

He tapped his pipe on the fireplace, opened the face of the clock, and adjusted the minute hand.

Long fingers, blunt-ended, oddly youthful.

A shiver went down my spine.

"Must you?" I nearly said.

CHAPTER 13

I have known far more exacting employers than Mr. Grant, who had the virtue of being patient with a learner. He always introduced unfamiliar subjects with a word of explanation, and demonstrated how small aspects fitted in to the larger background. I began with a considerable backlog, and this cleared, I felt less nervous, and was still kept busy. I was coping with quite a lot of work which ordinarily went to the City. It kept me occupied and I was lulled into a sense of false security.

My real mistake was to decide the underlying tensions of our original interview were entirely of my own manufacture. If I isolated Mr. Grant and disciplined memory firmly, there was no difficulty at all. In a brusque sort of way, he was harmless, treating me with consideration, but maintaining a very accurate arm's length. Soon I relaxed and began to enjoy the many comforts of my new life.

Whatever Aunt Anglesey thought, I'd done a sensible thing. I felt aggressively healthy; the children were quiescent; money ceased to be a bogey. My employer was often in London, overnighting at his club, and I could put him out of mind for long periods. If he returned late, he usually went straight to his room. He was frail, and hardly equal to his day. At any time, he retired early.

I was surprised, therefore, when he settled down with me in the library after dinner, in what seemed an unusually communicative mood. I had learned to inquire about share indexes and the peculiarities of world-trade in jargon I had chiefly connected with the Chancellor of the Exchequer. I thought I was doing very well, but he changed the subject.

"How are you liking it here, Mrs. Brandon? Now you're established, it's not so painful surely?"

"Quite the reverse," I said politely. "I do so enjoy the magic arrival and departure of food. I used to skimp meals, and anyhow, commuting took away any appetite."

"I'm glad I was right. I hope you appreciate my insistence. We are even moderately *compatible,*" he mocked the word slightly, "in a strictly class-conscious sort of way."

"Meaning what?"

"The demure, downcast eye, meek and rather shifty. The chimney-corner retreat, the Victorian stitching. You have a grim determination to keep your place, Mrs. Brandon."

"Of course. Would you have it otherwise?"

"I don't know," he said.

"I do. My job, after all, is merely to maintain the prevailing clockwork efficiency and disturb everyone as little as possible. I don't expect to be here for long."

111

"Why? Are you intending to leave me so soon?"

"Actually I was thinking of your own domestic circumstances. One senses the wind of change."

"What makes you say that?"

"You have obviously a very charming future, Mr. Grant."

He laughed. It was a short bark he had acquired.

"You're a diplomat, I see. You do have a lot of virtues. But is that an oblique question? If so, I'll ask another. Do you like Carolyn?"

"She's delightful. You're a lucky man."

"And Elvira? Would you recommend her as a mother-in-law? I thought I noticed you didn't like her."

"My grim determination, Mr. Grant, to keep my place, precludes me from discussing your friends with you."

"Pure Brontë! How you can, Mrs. Brandon! Yet you do it so well."

I thrust my needle viciously into a peony of noble proportions, overblown as Elvira herself. "I hardly know them anyway."

"But by and large you recommend the marriage?"

"I'm your secretary," I snapped, "not your amatory adviser."

He laughed again with far more genuine amusement. Not that I looked up.

"Come now, why shouldn't you offer me amatory advice? Everyone else does."

"I'm not interested."

"But that's just what I need. Most of my mentors are so prejudiced. Now you have a neutral temperament, and besides are a self-declared employer-hater. I shall value your opinion."

It was not a challenge I should have ordinarily considered, but I was afraid too great a show of reluctance would be misconstrued. Then too, I was sufficiently annoyed not to trust myself with a snub or a haughty rejoinder. I adopted a judicious air.

"Knowing nothing of the situation, I can't attempt advice. Carolyn is young, beautiful, and seems intelligent as well. Obviously she's devoted to you. You're older, of course, and a widower, but I assume you're now over the mourning period, though you still miss the companionship. It must be lonely in this big house. You fall in love again. There's your solution."

"You are indeed ignorant," he replied coolly. "I neither miss nor mourn my wife. I disliked her almost pathologically. For choice, I prefer to live alone. As for Carolyn. What makes you think I'm in love with her?"

I abandoned my peony and stared at him incredulously. He was shadowed by his deep wing chair, so that I had to focus on the illuminated prisms of the cut glass in his hand. Beyond, the face was screened and enigmatic, the eyes half-closed. It was an impression of disconcertingly familiar fingers, and thick, short lashes equally unaffected by age.

"If you have no feeling for the girl," I replied coldly, "these questions surely answer themselves."

"Not entirely. I must put you in the picture. We'll have a cool, academic discussion, suited to your detachment. The Linley-Morgans are people with the simplicity of a balance sheet—theirs being habitually in the red. When the old man died, his money went to his second, younger family. Carolyn has to marry well; she's been softly reared in days of generous alimony. You can't blame her if she prefers the devil she knows. It's easier to call it a prospective business deal. On my side, I need a wife so I can have a son. I'm a man with only one ambition—obsession if you prefer it. Obviously an injection of health, youth and strength is biologically desirable, and one is prepared to pay for it. I may well be over-ambitious but that's the luck of the game."

The statement of accounts, quietly, flatly delivered, shook me badly. Women prefer such matters decently clothed in sentiment, or else they do not mention them at all. But worse, here was that one-track mind; I knew it so well. Ruthless, riding rough-shod; Mike's father, Ronan's son. Thank heaven, an heir is a legitimate creation! Looked at like that the menace dwindled.

"What a very odd discussion," I said coldly.

"I can see you think happiness an essential ingredient of marriage," he continued with the same detachment. "I consider it relative. My second marriage couldn't be more deplorable than my first, and meanwhile I've been well-conditioned. Besides, from what I know of Carolyn, she'd be less vocal than Faith about my shortcomings. No one certainly could be more so. She needn't lack alternative amusements with that face and figure, and her mother will insure she's discreet. Offhand, the arrangement seems ideal."

I was trying to estimate the exact damage to personality. It was difficult for me to visualize what chronic ill-health, or marital failure, could do to a man like Ronan, proud, idealistic, and with hypersensitive areas of vanity. My own lot had not been easy, but I'd been physically tough and in day to day contact with youth and illusion.

Youth—yes. And now Carolyn, who was the same age as Mike, was separated from this married man by more than years. If, as I believed, she had something of my temperament, he mustn't be allowed to do this. One pawn could be protected, if I could only find the gambit.

"She's sufficiently handicapped as it is," my thoughts emerged into speech. "That woman for a mother, a divorce behind. I get the impression she's in a muddle, and I'm certain she doesn't know what she's doing. It would be bad enough if she weren't fond of you, but she has a *thing*—you can see that. I'm afraid she thinks of you in terms of paternal protection; the kindly older man. How ironic! You can't do this to her. You'd maim her irrevocably.

"You must learn if you ask for an opinion, you sometimes get one. I don't like the age gap; I don't like the health gap. But all this could be, and sometimes is, irrelevant. Common interests, mutual ambitions, real, generous affection, can bridge enormous chasms. Or adoration and passion can move mountains, temporarily at least. If you want to marry the child, you could at least try to love her; if you can't, then leave her to someone who can."

"You think one can love to order?"

"I think you're a taker, not a giver, Mr. Grant."

"I should say rather I'm incapable of the happy medium."

He rose and helped himself to another drink. I vaguely noted this was his third, and rather larger than his habit. *In vino veritas?*—for I couldn't remember if whisky occurred in Latin! But when he offered me one too, I accepted. Unwise perhaps, but I was beginning to feel milled by this grinding conversation.

"I offer what Linley-Morgans demand—ease and material comfort. I don't criticize them. Women are queer animals anyhow. They will go to remarkable lengths to satisfy subconscious needs, distorting any emotional picture to suit their taste. I don't pretend to understand the breed. Take you yourself, Mrs. Brandon. You applied for a job you didn't want; and took it too, under very light persuasion. To me, that is a very interesting example of female psychology."

He knew exactly how and where to hit; I adjusted my guard quickly.

"Not nearly so puzzling as why you engaged me under the circumstances."

"I could think of several reasons. I could be a masochist."

"It would explain why, when I try to behave conventionally, you prod me deliberately into impertinence."

115

"That occurred to me too. I'm sorry to be uncooperative, but I really dislike you too much."

"I'm sorry too. I like you very well . . . too well . . . I do find your opinions so refreshing. I'm sure you could influence me for the better. You've already proved I should make a very limp and unsuitable husband for Carolyn. Good! We'll throw the fish back in the water."

"But you can't! It's too late. That would hurt her too in a different way."

"My dear Mrs. Brandon, you must be more consistent. You say yourself I'm incapable of loving her or anyone else. I don't deny it. A quiet ghost walks. Carolyn was only jogging a memory, best left buried. You say she's beautiful. The camouflage of youth. It soon rubs off with hard wear. You were once a pretty slip of a girl yourself, perhaps. A lure for the unwary; more adventurous than now."

"I've certainly got over adventure at my age," I said pointedly.

"Your age. I wonder what it is? I shouldn't have thought you much older than I am. The right side of fifty anyway."

It's absurd, I know, but it was like a slap in the face. Ridiculous it should be the little, trivial things which cause betrayal. Without second thoughts, I rose to the bait:

"I'm forty-one," I retorted coldly.

I suppose one always nurses the small hurt to screen infinitely more complex emotions. How unwise! The inherent bravado of vanity. I should never have stood my ground, far too near him, a prickly kitten staring the bigger enemy in the face. His eyes began to wrinkle at the corners. Then worse, I watched that single dimple reemerge faintly from its long hiding-place and slowly deepen. Years sloughed themselves away. His characteristic smile was durable—and unendurable.

I faced the truth. I'd come to look for this Ronan, and I

had found him. Serve me right. Who'd have believed a mature woman could have behaved so stupidly. Incredible I should have thought him changed. Now, I'd have known him anywhere.

"Is it possible," he inquired, and to make matters worse, he dropped back into the old lilt I remembered so well, "is it conceivable Mrs. Brandon had no idea why I engaged her? Ach, but she's attractive for forty-one—no doubt about that! Just the person to console me for departed matrimonial ambitions. A really generous reformer, as I'm sure you are, might even feel it her duty. Do you never smile?"

By that time, I was moving in a thick mist, and was too blinded to be far short of panic. My only recognizable wish was to cry like a silly baby. I had reached some pitch of exasperation, so angry and muddled, I avoided even dignity. That he should dare to flirt openly with his middle-aged secretary, was a final, dreadful insult to the wretched girl of long ago. I seemed to be suffering from some triple split of personality; it was difficult to reclaim Mrs. Brandon.

He took a step nearer and dropped his hands on my shoulders. His actual touch broke my trance. It was more than could be borne. I graduated from long apathy to fiery circulation without transition. I couldn't stand it.

"Keep your hands off me, Mr. Grant!" I whipped out of reach as though bitten by a poisonous reptile. My voice went very quiet but very clear. I hardly recognized it. "What makes you think you're irresistible? It would take longer than Miss Wilk's six years to reduce me to doting status. I have better things to do than satisfy your vanity. Find yourself some easier game. And remember please, what is due to a subordinate under your roof. Though not, thank God! for much longer. I give you notice here and now."

"I wasn't actually going to seduce you, Mrs. Brandon."

"It never occurred to me you could," my temper was right

117

out of hand now, glorious and pain-killing. "You haven't the cut of a caveman."

"Is that your requirement?" It infuriated me that his self-control was absolute. He was sharp-featured, ice-cold, very collected.

"There's a happy medium," I said.

I could have bitten out my tongue. I made him wince. I shouldn't have done that. It was momentary, though I saw it. He recovered almost immediately. He'd always been like that, Ronan. Easy to hurt, quick to shrug it off.

"I'm sorry my shortcomings are so blatant, Mrs. Brandon. I do sympathize with you. And I am delighted that in this, at least, you can be candid and truthful."

"Goodnight!" I nearly shouted. It was a physical effort to turn away from him, even more difficult not to run to the door when it beckoned me. The stairs were different. I took them two at a time. It was hours before I hammered any sense into my head. Only one truth was clear. It must never happen again. I daren't even be alone with him. It was more than flesh and blood could thole. Mr. Grant was one person, Ronan another.

CHAPTER 14

Next morning, when I went down to breakfast with eyes as heavy as my dread, I learned with tremendous relief that not only would *M'sieur* keep to his room till lunchtime, but that the Linley-Morgans were due at midday to form a party for a point-to-point. I could not concern myself, as did Si-

mone, that in such a wind, *M'sieur* would undoubtedly catch
a chill and have to keep his bed for days. It might even be a
solution. . . . There was a natural reluctance to disappear
into thin air. I was by disposition a scrupulous employee.

I sat next to Elvira at lunch and amazed her by my fever-
ish and importunate conversation. She snubbed me once;
she snubbed me twice; but still I came up for more. Ronan,
at the head of the table, surrounded by country neighbours
seldom perhaps glanced in my direction, but I wished to insure that if he did, he would see me poised and careless. I
didn't look at him. I couldn't turn him back into Mr. Grant
anymore.

It is some measure of my skulking that, overhearing voices
on the landing, I actually hid rather than face him.

"You don't look a bit well, Ronnie," Carolyn was saying
anxiously. "Honestly—do you think you're up to it?"

"It's going to pour." This was Elvira. "You really should
cry off; no one would mind. Why not stay indoors by the fire.
Carolyn can keep you company."

"The air will do me good. I have a headache."

As often happens, more people returned than had set out.
I kept out of the way. The accent was on youth and things
sounded lively in the drawing room. Annette was in her ele-
ment, bouncing about happily. The record player throbbed
mechanically, and drinks began to flow.

"Can I help you, Annette?" I asked.

"But no, Madame. I manage ver' well. I am a bar girl, yes?
Meeswilk, she does not know to mix even the Martini, so
sometime she do the beds to assist. That would save much
time, Madame, if you do not mind."

I liked the idea of being upstairs and out of the way. I
soon finished the guest rooms and proceeded rather more reluctantly to that of the host. I didn't wish to be anywhere
that smacked too much of Ronan.

I'd never seen his bedroom. I didn't want to. Such silliness, however, is inexcusable. I squared my shoulders, opened the door, and switched on the light.

"For Heaven's sake, Annette! Turn the bloody thing off!"

I did so like a reflex. It hadn't occurred to me he might have left the drawing room. The glow of the electric fire showed him lying across the bed, his hand now shielding closed eyes. There was even a possibility he need not notice his error.

"And shut the window when you draw the curtains," he continued. "That damned row! They must all be deaf downstairs."

Obedience was obviously the least suspicious course, and when I had shut out the carriage light from the drive, I moved in deep shadow. I had already changed into a black dress.

"That's better!" he approved. "And now if you'd bring me a glass of water, *ma petite,* I'll swallow some more of these horse-balls. And incidentally, I'll be down for dinner."

I was probably unnaturally silent, but I had a sporting chance, even so, for he turned away to select a pill from the far table, taking the glass from me as he did so. His hand was shaking badly and it fumbled against mine. As we touched, he swivelled slowly round.

"I'm upstairs maid tonight," I apologized. "Is there anything else I can do for you, Mr. Grant?"

He returned the tumbler, and again his hand brushed mine. I was too busy coping with the resultant electric shock to reply.

"After last night I wouldn't dare to ask you even to rub cologne on my temples. You'd say I had designs on your virtue."

Before I could stop myself, I giggled. It was a misleading

atmosphere. In that vague, diffused light-glow, his hair was uncompromisingly black again, his face a familiar blur.

"*Touché!*" I said. "By the way, what's the matter with you?"

"Nothing. I get this damned neuralgia, more on than off, all the time. Depends where it hits me how I stand up to it. It's happened before, and will happen again. Anyhow, it's easing off now. I'm at the stage when I rejoice in contemplating all that is gloomy and unpleasant."

"Not very good psychology."

"I have to think of last night anyway. That music hammers it into my head. You were right about Carolyn, of course. I've never even danced with her."

"Rather an irrelevant comment."

"Not really. Do you know last time I danced was nineteen-forty? She wasn't even born. A club in a cellar with a transparent floor. The light came up through paving stones of many-coloured glass. I forget what the place was called. I remember only its stained white radiance. Did you know London during the war?"

"I mostly lived in the country."

"She was a good dancer . . . she was no weight at all. I could carry her easily. I often did. She was rather like you, Mrs. Brandon, or should I say, I imagine a resemblance? It might excuse me. Believe me, it's a compliment. She was so lovely. Life, to be sure, is nothing much to lose, but young men think it is. . . . Lord! I'm rambling. A sign my dope's working."

"Wouldn't you like to go to sleep?" I asked hastily in an unsteady voice.

"No," he replied. "I'd far rather tell you the story of my life. A bore for you perhaps but you did ask if there was anything you could do. Well, you can listen. It might even amuse you to hear how the biter was bit, by what is, I think, known as your 'physical type.' Hence, perhaps, my amatory miscalculation."

"I'm sorry about last night, Mr. Grant. I lost my temper."

"Once upon a time, Mrs. Brandon, I could have satisfied even you with the nobility of my sentiments. For I was the Galahad breed—would you credit it? I dreamed of a Grail. Oddly enough, I found one. It had a body, a face, two arms, and do you know?—the actuality was more wonderful than the ideal. Balboa had nothing on me. He only gazed into the Pacific. Did he drown in it too, I wonder? But he was a man. I was only a boy."

"Young people soon learn to swim," I said drily.

"How right! You make him sound foolish, that youngster of twenty-two. You'll say he ought have known better. I hardly like to tell you how it happened. You're a woman of the world. You won't believe anything so stupid. I found her walking the East End streets and took her home with me. I made love to her. She gave me every encouragement. Small cause for worshipping the very ground she walked on, but I needed something to worship, needed it badly. I suppose that's the explanation.

"I must be fair. She wasn't the usual type of pickup. Impossible to sort out at this distance, what truth there was in her story. Easier to say that I was a lamb for the slaughter— in more ways than one. For I was marked with the sign of death like something out of Sherlock Holmes. She could safely bury me when the interlude was over. I understand her point of view now. I didn't always. You see, I used to believe she loved me as I loved her.

"But I didn't exactly die. A miracle happened . . . the outside chance . . . a million to one. And this is the extraordinary thing: I thought it had been given me because she needed me. Did you ever hear such a ridiculous idea? There

I was in the hands of the Gestapo! Knowing what I do now, I'd be wiser, girl or no girl. She cost a lot in endurance and shame."

"She couldn't know that," I protested.

"No. But I do. However, time passed. I wouldn't dream of boring you with all my adventures. It was a long progress, toward peace and home, but I still believed in myself and my love. For her, I survived in the most impossible circumstances. I was nearing her; I'd see her again; it was enough. She needed me; she was mine; I honestly believed it.

"Fortunately, I was unconscious when I finally touched down on British soil, or I do believe I'd have looked for her. She ought to have been there . . . waiting! I remember being surprised she wasn't at my bedside when I came round. I might have known. She was married, after all. She'd even got a baby. But at last I could make inquiries, luckily very tactful ones. No one need ever know what a fool I'd been. She'd gone back to her husband; she'd had two more children. Three of them! So domesticated! Only I didn't laugh then. I looked at myself instead. I admitted for the first time what a mess I was; I faced that the future was a blank. Poor girl, she certainly had a skeleton in her cupboard, it was no idle metaphor. So I slammed the door on it.

"And there you are, Mrs. Brandon. It didn't take long did it? I was lucky that money came my way, but it couldn't buy health and youth, as you know. As for my black-out girl, who cares all these years afterwards? I suppose she's alive somewhere, with false teeth maybe, and varicose veins. I don't want to meet her. I never did know her married name. I'd rather she didn't know that I, at least, never loved again— no one, not even myself. She and the war did a thorough job between them. There's nothing left of me at all."

I had often wondered how it felt to take punishment, left to the body, right to the jaw, till you drooped against the ropes. Michael often watched fights on television and even my innate dislike of violence gradually gave way to curiosity. Michael! Remember him! He was the trophy. If you managed to avoid a knockout, you could sometimes win miraculously on points.

"Poor girl!" I smiled. "You're rather hard on her, for as far as I can see, she had no reason to suppose you came back for her. And now, Mr. Grant, I really must go. Take my advice. Dismiss the past and take a look at the present. It has a sort of peace, compared with war. Are you sure you'll be down to dinner?"

Long after I had left him, I was haunted by *l'esprit de l'escalier,* and his quiet, sub-acid narrative echoed in my ears. She was vulnerable too; she was young. She knew more about loving than he did. Forgotten more than he would ever learn. But in his own way, he had paid tribute too. Aunt Anglesey was wrong; I was right. The thought gave me no particular consolation.

Dinner passed uneventfully; we were still at opposite ends of the table. He looked ill, but he was making an unusual effort to be pleasant and gay. Afterwards I made for the seclusion of the library, only to be interrupted before I could fall into sentimentality again.

"I thought Mr. Grant might be here."

I wouldn't have chosen Elvira Linley-Morgan for a companion at that particular juncture. The faint fumes of cocktails drifted past, and I had already noticed she was a garrulous drinker.

"He looked ghastly at dinner." She was plaintive. "I told Car . . . she ought to have got things settled. He's in for a new bout now. I can tell the signs. It would obviously be better if Car took him to his house in the Bahamas so he could have a rest, and not come back till summer. These attacks are cropping up far too often. Faith always said it was a bad sign. Mind you, she never thought he'd last this long. Something to do with pressures on the brain from some injury when the Germans were banging him around. Some doctor told him it might take years to find out what was really wrong. Cheerful prospect! And getting worse all the time."

Quite untroubled, she removed her exotic evening sandals and paused to wriggle her fat toes ecstatically.

"That's much better!" she remarked. "Now where were we?"

"Burying Mr. Grant," I said.

She laughed. She had too many teeth.

"As long as we see Car's the widow," she continued. "Oh, he's always in and out of hospital, but it's only a temporary measure. If they really sorted him out, they'd kill him. I knew Faith Grant well, of course. Silly girl! Why make a fuss with all that money dropping in her lap? Ronnie's shortcomings at every bridge table. In bed and out of it. You know the type."

"But a useful guide when it comes to choosing a husband for your daughter, Mrs. Linley-Morgan. Unhappy marriage can become a habit."

"She could do far worse." She shrugged. "And the stupid child has no interest in doing better. Never looks at an eligible young man twice. Of course, he has no heirs, but that doesn't mean she'll get it. Besides, married to him, she's more chance to get him out of her system."

I couldn't help feeling vaguely sick, listening to her talking like that about a girl of twenty—and Ronan!

"If he's so ill, and knows it, maybe he doesn't want to marry," I tried.

"He's no right to, but he wants his precious heir so badly it'll drive him to it."

You could see that anyone living at close quarters with

Elvira might well become money-conscious. I hadn't till then really registered that Ronan had no conceivable heirs. Thank Heaven, I'd kept my head so far, and it would soon be over!

But the same instinct which turned my thoughts to my children included Carolyn.

"She's under age," I said aloud, rather thoughtfully. "The whole thing sounds quite appalling to me, from everyone's point of view."

"Shades of Miss Wilk?" She fixed her blue, gimlet gaze upon me.

"Not necessarily," I replied coolly. "You might well find me a worthier antagonist."

"Indeed? So that's the way the wind blows, Mrs. Brandon? How amusing! Miss Wilk regretted her interference. I wonder what you think you can do."

"You'd be surprised!" I said sweetly.

And I'd see she was!

CHAPTER 15

I was cheered by my altercation with Elvira. She could be trusted to tell tales at first opportunity, and her timing was almost bound to be inappropriate. Next day, Ronan took the Linley-Morgans with him into London, leaving me mercifully alone for two or three days. I was able to confirm my notice in writing, finish off my work, and even do the bulk of my packing. I also reminded myself of stern duty, in case it escaped my mind. Geoffrey, Renata, Michael, these three; and most particularly, Michael.

I was a sensible middle-aged woman. I was also a mother.

It must have been the Wednesday when, aching after a long, damp walk, I retired early with a paperback full of bullet holes. The first chapter was certainly promising, but that's all I can remember. I was next jerked wide awake by a sense of something amiss. I was cold and stiff with unexpected sleep, and no wonder! It was after midnight.

Something *wrong;* that jungle feeling; every woman knows it. The antennae quiver. Renata had her appendix; Mike, a friend with a vicious sportscar; as for Geoffrey—was he really looking well? *Wrong;* had I perhaps heard something, and not so far away either? Fire? Burglars? That reminded me. I'd left my handbag in the library, alone and unprotected. I must get it at once!

I scrambled into my Anglesey dressing gown, almost fumbling with its ridiculous bows. Outside, there was no sign of smoke, no smell of burning, probably no burglars either! Just the same, I'd feel happier with my bag, and sleep better for its company.

The house was very still. A full moon was centered in the arched window; it cast eerie shadows, spotlighted irrelevant detail. The exquisite, curved balustrade, the wide sweep of stairway was silvered and formal as the scenery of an old ballet. Instinctively, I floated, velvet and chiffon flying behind me, my fingertips sliding smoothly down the rail. I moved in a stage scene, feeling an almost histrionic pleasure.

Was I still sleep-dazed? Was I carried a little beyond reality as the moonbeams thronged on the dark stair, and I reached the empty hall?

My bare foot caught on something soft and the nightmare was back. I pitched forward wildly.

I'd never fallen over a body before. Live burglars were bad enough. Dead ones beyond anything. My teeth chattered until I managed to clamp them together. Then I heard the

breathing, rough and retching in the stillness. I pulled myself together and turned.

He lay in shadow, sprawled across the last tread, spilling
on to the cold black-and-white flagstones. A hand clutched
the final bannister and I noted the rhythmic contraction of
the forearm, expressing some ultimate of pain. In the dim
light, his face had a grey, fearful luster and his features were
meaningless, cancelled out by the struggle behind them. He
was a thing, not a man, but he belonged to me.

I dropped down beside him and pulled him roughly
against me, cradling him like a big child, smoothing his
sweat-damp hair.

"Ronan," I called him. "Oh my love, my dear one!"

Clumsily, he transferred his tourniquet grip to my forearm where it remained, numbing but reassuring. If we held
each other grimly enough, he couldn't come to any harm; I'd
protect him against anything—*anything!* It was the only
idea I could muster.

"Ronan! Ronan!" Once started, I couldn't stop. I repeated
the name with every variation of endearment, very softly.
It used to be called crooning but the word has become de-
based.

No sense came into my head till I felt his slight relaxation,
and a gulping breath that ended in a weary sigh. I let out a
panic wail, only the word doctor recognizable.

"Sit still!" he ordered in a difficult, muffled voice.

"Ronan, I've done everything wrong—perhaps killed you.
You must let me get help."

In the hollow of my shoulder, his head shook economi-
cally.

"But you're *hurt!*"

"No!" he said. "And don't fidget."

I continued to sit in what gradually became intense discomfort but the Yoga effect was sobering, and I noted his breathing had eased and his grip was less convulsive.

"You should be somewhere warm . . . you must be put to bed . . . I must get Simone . . . you must go to hospital . . . see a doctor. . . .

"You haven't broken your neck?"

"Nothing so exciting. Do relax."

"But this doesn't happen all the time?"

"Too bloody often. I won't die on you."

"Can I do anything?"

"I ran out of tablets . . . couldn't make it . . . stumbled. You'll find some in the right-hand drawer of the desk. Red box . . . they're stronger."

When I returned, he was sitting on the stairs, his head in his hands.

"There's still a fire in the library. And a sofa."

"No." He spoke like a sick, rebellious child. "I want my bed."

I didn't like it. I hated to watch him pull upwards, angrily shaking off any help. I'd never noticed there were so many stairs; I remembered the landing was enormous.

"I'm only fit to live in a damned bungalow," he gasped.

The lights were on now. He was ashen with fatigue. He staved off unconsciousness till he reached his target.

I installed him in proper comfort. He couldn't protest.

"You're shivering, love. Put something round yourself. Sorry about all this, but I'm fine now."

"You're conscious? Thank heaven! Is there anything more I can do?"

"You could call me Ronan again."

"You heard me?"

"Of course, love."

"And you know who I am? Yes, I suppose so. I thought you might be too ill to notice."

"I wasn't quite dead! All that artistic keening. Not at all the style of the stern and virtuous Mrs. Brandon."

"Oh Ronan!" My tears could be postponed no longer and I bowed my head on his smooth linen sheet. He stroked my hair gently while I sobbed my heart out. I had rehearsed a possible unmasking so often; now I hardly noticed it had happened.

"What a daft thing to do, love. Did you honestly believe I could live with you, day in, day out, and never guess? Shame on you, Mari!"

"But you didn't recognize me at first. You know you didn't."

"Did you hate me for it? Darling, I am sorry. But be fair, love. Supposing I'd come to sell brushes at your door? You did mislead me, as you well know. And what have you done to your pretty hair? Mind you, I don't say I didn't admire the wretched Mrs. Brandon. There was something about her views on Commonwealth Trade which stirred the senses, and her nose was too small for those hideous spectacles."

"And she fell in love with Mr. Grant, despite the conditions of service."

"Are you sure? The other night when I was man enough to cope, you made your attitude very plain. I did think, if I touched you, it would be, well—like it used to be. But how you shuddered! It diminished me dreadfully. I felt less than I'd become, and that's bad enough. I seem to be as repulsive as I feel."

"You don't understand. I was frightened there was still so much blood left in me—recirculating. So you knew then?"

He nodded. "I wanted you to lose your temper, so I could be sure. I had to stop your playacting somehow. Otherwise you might just have been a sort of *Doppelgänger,* reminiscent enough to plague me and bring me to life again—for no good reason. I didn't want to replace you; I never have. But when

I'd proved my point, I still didn't know where we stood. I wondered why you'd come; why you, of all people, had deceived me. I asked what you wanted of me; it was quite clear what you *didn't* want! What could I do, but play a waiting game?"

I sidetracked. "Ronan, you're a devious Gael! You were trapping me all the time. And how dare you say those awful things about me? I did love you. You know I did."

"Past tense you see."

For answer, I looked down at him. It was a very dear face. I kissed the lurking, solitary dimple.

"One," I said irrelevantly. "I can't think why you only have one."

"One love too." He smiled. "But it's an elegant sufficiency."

The conversation deteriorated. What a strange pair! A sick man in his bed; a middle-aged woman at her worst in the early hours of the morning. We returned to the flat in Regent's Park. The past was safe; its detail comforting. We raked for happiness. The past tense. We needed to ratify the old enchantment.

I stayed beside him for a long time, anxiously watchful even after his absurd, doll's eyelashes finally settled on his pale cheeks. He had a faint, relaxed smile, as he slept as though his small tribute to half-forgotten grace and beauty had subtly eased him.

I forget my thoughts—if I had any. It was enough to have Ronan again.

Annette had to shake me.

"It is near one o'clock, Madame."

"Oh Lord!" I woke befuddled. "Why did you let me sleep so long?"

131

She showed her pointed, kitten's teeth. "This is the orders, Madame. *M'sieur,* he say you must rest for he disarrange you last night with the *crise*. We see it coming since many days."

"How is he this morning?"

"Today, all is well. He says he's fine, though it is not true. And he want you when you finish lunch. He tell me three times."

I'm ashamed to say, I studied myself in the mirror. It told me very little. The one person you cannot see is yourself. Nevertheless, for the first time in years, I really took trouble over my appearance. On my way to Ronan's room, I added still more flourishes, and blushed at my own foolishness.

He was lying on a daybed in front of a proper fire, but he got up when I entered. He greeted me with the awkward eagerness of a boy.

"Here you are! Darling, I was almost frightened you wouldn't come. You look wonderful. All this and Elizabeth Arden too. How old are you? Nineteen?"

"The right side of fifty," I retorted.

"Why so am I! What a coincidence!"

We were shy. I don't know why older love is less arrogant, more self-conscious, even a little straitlaced.

"You don't look too bad after such a rough night."

"I'm upright again, which is unusual the first day. You must be the medicine I need. Come here."

He reached out for me uncertainly, and I went to him hesitantly. We stood, cheek against cheek, slowly relaxing, taking time to catch up with the years of loneliness. We didn't speak for a long time. We didn't want to. It was a deeply important moment. Tenderness has a very thawing quality—and how rarely we are asked to give or receive it.

"It's like going home, love," he said at last in a shaken voice. "Oh my dear one! You always were my peace."

Poor Ronan! How could I possibly love him less, now he

needed me as he'd never done before? There didn't seem to be much future, but he owned the present at least.

"Is that what they call *tisane?*" I asked about a concoction Simone brought. "It reminds me of Aunt Anglesey's brews."

"Do you honestly mean you told Mrs. Anglesey about us? How could you? She terrifies me. I think of her as Fate. I used to play a game. She was the agency which would bring us back together, if it were the right thing. I must have been quite mad. But you see it happened in the end. It took a long time though."

"Twenty years," I marvelled.

"Twenty-two to be precise. Less, of course, since I saw your aunt. I went to announce my marriage and close the account."

"Yes, she told me about it."

"Why the hell didn't you leave your husband, love? I'd have come to you, only too quickly; we'd have managed somehow."

Ronan was special. But I found I owed it to John not to strip him down in front of his triumphant rival when he could no longer defend himself. He had fathered my children. He had protected Ronan's son. We had been husband and wife in our fashion.

"Not knowing you were there, I stuck to my side of the bargain, and got along as best I could."

"Happily?"

"It wasn't too bad," I replied.

Quite early in the evening, Ronan began to flag, and to tell the truth I myself felt like a sprinter tackling the Olympics without first going into training.

"It doesn't wax cauld," I remarked defiantly.

"No, love," he mocked me, "but it waxeth bloody tiring!"

"I suppose you 'want your bed,'" I teased him. "Well, no stairs this time, thank Heaven."

"I must kiss you goodnight first. I think I'm scared—are you? It can't be the same, can it? Do we try?"

"Why not?" I probably sounded dubious too.

"I don't want to spoil things. Silly, isn't it?"

"Between you and me, Ronan? Yes."

We needed have worried. It was nothing to do with our lost fortnight, but it was part of belonging. Curiously passionless too. I was surprised Ronan looked dazed.

He held me at arm's length and stared at me puzzled.

"Oh my God!" he muttered. "What have I done? So help me! What have I done?"

"What's the matter?"

"You'd better go. I've had enough. There *is* tomorrow."

Next day, I was to discover that Ronan's prowess owed much to carefully administered drugs and the excessive use of willpower. He looked wretched when I went in to see him, and he was still in bed.

"I don't usually get up the first day," he admitted ruefully. "I'm paying for it."

"I'm sorry. I encouraged you."

"But it was fine, wasn't it? The right thing to do? I didn't let you down altogether? And now I mustn't crack up on you either. Let me sleep off the effects, and I'll be in better form by this evening."

I must have been overdue some sleep myself for I dozed off in the afternoon by the library fire, and resented being roused almost at once by a hysterical Simone.

"Madame, Madame!" she wailed, and burst into headlong French, too fast to follow.

Fortunately, Annette joined us then, though she, too, was gabbling.

"I cannot help this. I stop her but she push me—so! She is ver' angry. Already she is in the room of *M'sieur*. He is asleep but she wake him. I hear him say: 'Carolyn!' "

Simone took over. She wrung her hands histrionically. "He takes many of the pills. He will not be well. He should not wake. Madame, you must bring her away."

By now I had absorbed the situation, and, in my relief, found it funny.

"I thought Mr. Grant had had a relapse at least," I interrupted. "If Miss Linley-Morgan, an old friend, visits him, it's none of our business. Who's looking after his bell? They may want tea."

I gradually persuaded them back on duty, and returned to my own meditations. How could Carolyn have slipped my mind so completely? I felt guilty. Yet the situation had not been such that I could have inquired of Ronan how his matrimonial affairs had progressed. Now I wondered.

It must have been half-an-hour later that Carolyn herself pushed open the door and slammed it behind her.

"Well, Mrs. Brandon?" She opened attack at once. "Aren't you just too damned clever?"

"Meaning exactly what, Carolyn?"

"I might have known." She ignored my question. "He's been different all along. Not that it occurred to me *you* could have been the cause. If you only knew how you looked! That fantastically dowdy hat! I was staggered when I laughed and he stared at me. Then when you came down here, Mother said something . . . and he snapped her head off. Even so, I didn't register. When he behaved like cold mutton, I just thought he was ill. To have been jilted—and for you! I just can't believe it."

"I haven't heard the word jilted for years," I said to gain time.

"It's not exactly *with it,* but there's no other."

"It's not used as a rule without a formal engagement, or at least a proposal of marriage."

"I suppose you don't believe he's ever asked me but he did.

135

And I was fool enough to refuse. I couldn't help it. He took me by surprise. And he made it sound . . . oh, I don't know . . . a sort of bargain. Not at all how I'd imagined it. I needed time to think it over. Ronnie's so much older, and Mother and her friends are always whispering his sex life or something. I wasn't sure."

"First reactions are often the best guide."

She paid no attention. My presence wasn't really necessary. It seemed wise that she should get it out of her system. "We were still friendly," she continued, "but nothing happened. I made up my mind, but he didn't bring it up again. So I consulted Mother, fool that I was! She made a fuss, of course; said I didn't know which side my bread was buttered. She went on and on about money. It makes you feel uncomfortable, even if you don't show it. She knew I'd always had a *thing* about Ronnie. Even when I was little I hated Faith Grant. She was so big and pink and sarcastic. But he was kind. When my father went off with that woman, he was good to me."

"I do understand, Carolyn."

"How could you? He's nice to children. No wonder he wants some of his own. I could have made him happy. Anyhow I love him. I always have. Some kids get a crush on a filmstar or pop singer, I always stuck to Ronnie, and when I grew up and began to go about, I still liked him better than lumping boys who talked sex till you could scream. I wouldn't have gone on refusing. It was only that I had to get used to the idea of marriage. It's different somehow."

"It is, Carolyn. Very different."

She laughed hysterically. "I suppose you think you'll get him. He only wants a family; nothing else will tempt him to the altar. Plenty of widows and suchlike have tried that game before. You can't win. You may get some pickings. I suppose you'd be glad of a bit of extra money."

"I suppose it's a waste of breath to defend my honour?"

"If you had any. I hope you haven't. You've been working like a beaver for him all the time. I see that now. I didn't believe Mother when she told me. Anyhow, I wish she'd keep out of my affairs. She thinks she got rid of old Wilk for me. As if she mattered!"

"Do try and pull yourself together, child, and talk like an adult. But since we're not mincing words, I'll say this. You're well out of marriage with Mr. Grant and the day will come when you thank high Heaven for your freedom. You don't love him; he's a father substitute. But you're not a child anymore. You must learn that while an older man can be an excellent instructor, the actual match is played out between equals. Meanwhile, no damage has been done. You haven't lost face. Or his love, for you never had it—not any version which would build a marriage. Ahead of you is someone who would otherwise have come too late. You'll meet him now, and walk more delicately because of the experience behind you. I know it's hard to believe, but you'll find I'm right."

"Smooth-tongued bitch!" You could see she was a person who rarely lost control; her venom stuck in her throat—or was it tears? I was hampered myself by having no idea what had passed between the two upstairs. I felt she had blown off sufficient steam.

"Enough!" I said sharply. "Try and behave yourself. Far from being the sort of woman you suppose, I devote my energies to my family, and if my daughter, big as she is, showed so little sense of dignity, I'd take a slipper to her without the slightest compunction. Do you think you're the only girl who's ever had an unhappy ending? You're *lucky*, Carolyn. The great thing about the wrong man is *not* to marry him. And incidentally, I'm not going to marry Mr. Grant either—just for the record."

"You'll get what you can out of him and then ditch him, I suppose. Well look out he doesn't do it first."

So that was Carolyn!

As soon as she had gone, I thought of a thousand better ways of dealing with her, but it was a difficult scene to have had with a relative stranger. I was staring at the fire, trying to judge the exact extent of her hurt, when Ronan came in, pale and convalescent in his darkest suit.

"Not a very quiet afternoon after all."

I sighed. "Carolyn? I had her too, and I mishandled her. She's very mixed up. Fancy having to go back to that Elvira woman with the slap still hurting! You never told me you'd actually proposed to her."

"Only to be rejected. Frankly, I took that as my cure. If she'd have been really fond of me, she'd have jumped at it. No, she's just taken a knock to her vanity, as we all must from time to time. She'll get over it."

"It's more, I think. She feels very alone. She's lost a valuable mooring. Of course, it shocked her to step aside to make way for someone so much older. Her instincts warned her, I daresay, that there was something odd in the situation. I feel guilty."

"Why on earth? They did the job themselves, very efficiently, and before there was any situation, as you call it. Originally, I showed some tact. After she'd turned me down, she still liked to go about with me. Very convenient. Pretty girl for me, someone she could talk to. Then the campaign started. Elvira to the fore and full of bludgeoning tactics. I couldn't make up my mind. I didn't really want to. Then you turned up and tipped the scales. It was the cue to drift out of the tangle politely—but would they let me? Do you know, she sent a letter to my club—an ultimatum? I daresay Elvira sat over the poor child with a whip, but there was only one reply—in black-and-white. I fled the country after

I'd posted it. You'll agree, surely, I was too ill for tragedy. Still am."

"I'm sorry. I'm nagging you."

He smiled. "I expect it from Mrs. Brandon. Darling, let's drink to the exit of the Linley-Morgans. The child will be all right, and well rid of me—you know that. As for heartbreak—what do they know of it, this generation? That railway station. Do you remember?"

"Do I not!"

"You were a gallant child. Not one tear; and a smile glued across your face. You were worth any loving."

"And now we're together again. It still seems unbelievable, doesn't it?"

He didn't wait for an answer.

CHAPTER 16

There is a limit to nostalgia; exceed it and the sugar turns saccharine. We had retraced our beginnings. The subject was outworn. Beyond it, our measuring rods became different, unconnected. I see now it couldn't have lasted. By the third day, the scales were rubbing off the moth wings. It was sad but inevitable.

At breakfast instead of immersing ourselves in the daily papers, we made stilted conversation, both wishing the other would be quiet. Outside it was a leaden, lowering day, far too warm for the time of year. In the garden, an early climber blazed against a gun-metal wall with the luminous intensity

of flourescent paint. I tried a few careful, amorous re-
marks and felt like Mrs. Pat Campbell playing bridge
at seventy.

Ronan laughed. "Never mind, Mitty. I feel the same. *Non
sum qualis eram.* I'm over-conscious this morning that your
boyfriend did, in fact, die, and the elderly executive Mrs.
Brandon disliked so much is *me.*"

"I have a hangover from over-conscientious gaiety," I admitted. "I doubt if you've changed as much as I have.
Women are like the English climate, mostly winter."

"I disagree. Years of illness and inadequacy have left their
mark on me. Now, you've kept your wide-eyed innocence
somehow. Youth lingers in you like the interesting, subtle
bouquet of a vintage wine. How's that for nine o'clock in the
morning?"

"I shouldn't have thought myself interesting."

"Challenging then. You always were. Or am I just pathologically possessive? I never had a very large part of you.
Ironical, that everyone else had more. Do you know, I used
to be most jealous of that baby?"

I poured myself another cup of tea to gain time. Up till
then, it had been unnaturally easy to keep my life in com-
partments, for this was the first time he had made any real
reference to my alter ego. What an odd man he was, when
you came to think of it! All that high romance, completely
shorn of any day-to-day detail. All that retrospect, concentrated on two weeks out of twenty-two years. I had given
him the barest facts of how I came to rediscover him, yet he
had asked for no more. I found he was watching me speculatively. He's a stranger, I thought irrelevantly. He has
nothing really to do with me.

"It occurs to me your Geoffrey is as old as I was when we
met. Extraordinary! One digests it only slowly. And the
others? What about them?"

140

I picked my way cautiously. "I've a girl, Renata, and another boy."

"Still expensive? But I suppose you're really quite well off. And that desperation for money was assumed. I remember you belonged to cushioned people."

It was funny enough to divert my attention. "I'm afraid you pay the bills, Ronan. Believe me, I need your enormous salary; there's precious little beyond it. I meant every word I said; this was an ideal job. I've been able to let my house too. I'm actually solvent. Good thing! As Geoffrey says, we're all too old to beg. Mind you, it's all right for him. He has his uncle's money. Not much, but enough to make him an architect."

"But your family?"

"Were an extravagant, impractical lot, even before their world disintegrated. Mother was left on her own version of the breadline. Peg helps her, of course. Aunt Anglesey stands surety for us, and very good she has always been. We'd never have got by, otherwise. John left very little. He didn't get much from his aunt. I think, after all, she must have known, or guessed. She was terribly anti-drink and I wasn't always there to put up a smoke screen."

"That too? I didn't realize. No wonder you can't forgive me. What a ridiculous situation! And I thinking I had nothing to offer you. When I came into the money . . . I did, of course, wish I hadn't been so precipitate, but it didn't occur to me you could be having such a rough time."

"Don't be absurd. It was nothing to do with you. And now, I'm nearly out of the wood, and the trees getting very large."

"Nevertheless, we must do something about it."

Mrs. Brandon raised her eyebrows. "I'm not a Linley-Morgan."

We moved into the library. Outside, the storm still threatened. I was reminded of the Croft.

"Do you ever go back to Scotland now?" I asked idly.

"In fact, I have a house in Wester Ross. Can't think why I bought it. I only went there once. It was a failure to end failures. Hills I couldn't climb, deer I couldn't stalk, my hands too shaky even for a shotgun. The only occasion I tried to walk, I was practically carried home by a patronizing ghillie."

"How about fishing?"

"And how do I get uphill? What do you know about Scotland and fishing?"

"I lived up there for ages, till after the end of the war. I chap tatties, sweep chimneys upside down, and know a Writer doesn't necessarily produce a book."

"Funny you should mention that, while talking of departed ambitions. Mother wanted me to be a Writer and step into my Uncle Alec's shoes. But with a name like Grant, I had what might be called an Advocacy Fixation. I believe I'd have stuck to my resolution too, given money and health at the right time. I've always regretted it like a loss. I suppose that's why I'd enjoy having a son, who could do all these lamented things on my behalf."

I took a deep breath; it seemed to come from my solar plexus. I controlled my hands by shoving them in my pockets. Up till then, I had avoided deliberate cheating. It was no longer possible.

"Ambition at remove," I said with commendable lightness. "I'm afraid children never measure up to their parents' plans for them."

The statement hovered round my ears. I had a fleeting vision of Mike, complete with lawyer's wig, climbing boots, and my best trout rod. Up till that moment, Ronan's heir had been a mere recipient of money-bags, a salve for physical vanity. It was strange to know he had all he needed, withheld from him.

"You speak feelingly," he said. His smile wasn't genuine. "I wouldn't know."

After that we agreed on silence.

From the lunch table we moved to the library for coffee. The storm gathered outside. More logs were put on the fire.

"Do we take a nap," Ronan inquired with a sudden edge to his voice, "or carefully select one of our pieces of the past?"

"How unfair! I'll tell you something about the past. I've helped you to lay its ghosts. You can start afresh now. When I've gone."

"What exactly does that mean?"

"My week's notice. A little longer and you'll be released. You'll get no more of me. We've had the best of this; you won't be sorry."

"Who said?"

"Ronan, we've justified and pardoned old acquaintance. We both needed that. You can be free of me now, and of that hell of a fortnight. You can open a new chapter."

"So I find a new brood-mare? Not again, love! Why not say you're tired of me? That I'm just a mangled wreck; no good to anyone, least of all you?"

"The re-play's over; pretty while it lasted, but only a form of self-indulgence. For God's sake let's face it and finish."

"What's wrong, love? I used to be a sort of husband, didn't I? You can tell me all about it, you know. I think you should."

I shook my head miserably. It was the one thing I feared, that he would shelter me again.

"Fashions change. We don't, *m'eudail*. Why do you want to be cured?"

I only saw his eyes. Beyond them was a man, not a boy. A lover shorn of age or tense—my complement. Let us possess one world . . . no other mattered. The disease was incurable.

What a fool I'd been! We two could never deal in less than truth, and why hadn't I known mature loving was larger than its humbler beginning? I'd tell him everything, of course. It would be difficult, but he'd understand . . . perhaps know what we should do . . . but not yet . . . not just yet!

For he was kissing me now with all the defiance of his mad career down the dual carriageway. The sudden access to passion and strength was startling, my own response disconcerting, and when we drew apart to breathe, we stared at each other, marvelling at our triumphant breakthrough. Words were no use at all. We had our own language.

On to this silent curtain scene Michael took his usual gate-crashing cue. He stood on the threshold and brought the storm into the room. His eyes were scornful, anger was in his fingertips. Our tentative ascent to the clouds was over, and we came down to earth without a parachute.

He began without overture. "So it seems that drunken Linley-Morgan girl was right. I have the car outside. You're going back to London. Now!"

Any embarrassment was throttled by his tone. Michael and I could always quarrel the others to a standstill, and often did.

"How dare you speak to me like that! And since when did I take orders from you, Michael?"

"Since when has it been necessary? But now it is. You will leave this house at once."

"Don't shout at me. And what are you doing here? Why aren't you at Cambridge?"

"News travels. Incidentally, I'm here with Geoffrey's sanction."

"And since when did Geoffrey sanction uncouth, impossible manners? You storm into a strange house; you behave so badly that even I, little as I expect, can still be astounded."

"Time enough for explanations," he replied coldly. "Now you're coming with me."

"Indeed? By force if necessary?"

I knew I must eventually obey him; the situation was shocking, and, worse, it was dangerous. There was no decision, no choice, no free will.

"I shall come with you," I continued icily, "when I'm ready, and meanwhile you will apologize to Mr. Grant for your boorish behaviour in his house. You seem to have taken leave of your senses."

"Apologize? I'm damned if I will! Mr. Grant must be made to realize that you have sons well able to protect their mother."

He took a couple of strides, far too near Ronan. The two were much of a height but the boy appeared to tower above the man.

It was necessary to look at last. Anger left me to be replaced by misery. Ronan was as white as the marble behind him. His hand, gripping the fireplace for support, shook though its knuckles were yellowed with the effort of control. Pain and awareness lay in every line of his face. And there stood his son, ignorant as a young bull, and equally destructive. The confrontation was hideous.

"You can treat that Carolyn woman as you please," he now addressed his father directly. "She's trash anyhow. But when one of your drunken castoffs points to my mother as a probable successor, then I assure you, I know exactly what to do, and it's not apologize. If you've done any harm to her, if you say a word to her discredit, if you have anything further to do with her whatsoever, believe me, I'll knock your teeth down your throat."

"Michael!" I begged.

"Keep out of this, Mother. Go and collect your luggage."

I had no intention of leaving the two together. In different ways, neither looked responsible for words or actions.

"We must go," I agreed. "But I'm appalled. You attack Mr. Grant, whom you can see is ill. And in front of a friend and employer, you insult me beyond belief. You will leave this room and this house at once. You'll wait for me in the drive, and while I pack, you'll take a grip on your deplorable temper. Not only do you behave like a savage, but you make a laughingstock of yourself before strangers and their servants. Get out before you're thrown out. I'll deal with you later."

He scowled at me; I waited. How far had he travelled from the disciplines of childhood? I was metaphorically unbuckling my belt. To my relief, he wavered, still looking angry, but slipping into mere rebellion.

"After you," he said, and held the door open pointedly.

I looked toward Ronan. He had moved. While others raged and ranted, he had said no word. He now stood with his back to us, rather more erect. I noticed he had moved Gavin's photograph. It lay face upwards on the desk.

"Goodbye." What an odd word it is! What does it mean? I'd never said it to him before.

He didn't answer. He was right. It was all too shocking for the formalities.

"Come on, Mother. No need to hang around."

I walked through into the hall. Black and white flagstones, ill met by moonlight. Why had I ever come back?

I had already prepared for retreat, so it didn't take long to finish off the job. My luggage was soon in the car where Michael sat, surveying the Bentley without obvious signs of impatience. I thought up a satisfactory story for Simone; Annette was out.

I had to return to the library—a pointless gesture when

all that was left of Ronan and me was the silly boy we'd created together. Bastard by name and nature. The sins of father—and mothers—coming back to roost. Protected from his origins, he'd none the less revenged himself pretty thoroughly.

The storm had moved on, but no sun came through the library windows. The clock ticked deliriously as it caught up with the present. Ronan's head was pillowed on his arms, his hands lay loosely in front of him, he noticed nothing.

It was difficult to turn finally and leave him. But what else could I do? Perhaps I could pray that he'd hate me. Yes, that was it! Hate to trickle through him, fury to revive him, so he could drive out and destroy the pact between us.

I went as silently as I'd come.

CHAPTER 17

It was characteristic of Michael that, having achieved his object, his mood changed completely. He was pleased with himself.

"I wish G. could have seen that Bentley. Makes you see red to think of it wasted on a tick like that."

I was silent. You can't exactly dislike a child you've borne and bred, but you can have a very good try.

"It must be terrific to drive."

"You're not doing so now," I pointed out coldly. "These lanes are narrow."

I returned to my meditations while he dropped speed and looked at me sideways. Why hadn't I told Ronan about him? It was quite unpardonable. No, it wasn't. Could I really have trusted him? And how, in practice, would one have set about the business?

"I suppose you're furious with me?"

"Only ashamed of you, Michael." It was true. What must his father think of him? Uncouth; uncivilized; an ill-bred puppy!

"Hell!" he exclaimed. "I'm sorry, Mother! But he had it coming to him!"

"Allowing you behave like a guttersnipe, Michael, need you talk like one too? Moderate your language in front of me; after all, you have such a regard for my saintly reputation."

"I behaved as any son behaves who finds his mother in a compromising situation."

"Compromising! Must you be pompous too? You made an exhibition of yourself in front of my employer, and lost me my job. You bullied an ill man, and insulted me. I'm so upset, I don't wish to discuss the matter further."

In fact, I much preferred to pursue my own thoughts. What had Michael seen? He could be expected to misinterpret any lingering aura of closeness, but actually, how sensitive was he?

"I'm not apologizing," he continued firmly. "I meant every word. You don't seem to realize. People are talking about you—living with a man like that."

"Do you mean living in the same house—or something more? I like accusations clearly defined. Have I been seduced by Mr. Grant on his sickbed? Or have you successfully snatched me—a brand from the burning?"

"You shouldn't talk like that."

"Why not? Crude conversation is infectious. Incidentally, whatever mud you fling at Mr. Grant spatters me too. And what's all this about Carolyn?"

"Little bitch! It's a long story."

"I'm quite accustomed to being bored by my children, and we have at least an hour's journey to while away."

"You'll have to know sometime." He had the grace to look embarrassed. "It seems the only way to bring you to reason. You asked why I was in London. I came up for Julian's twenty-first . . . a party in his parents' flat. A key girl called off. I said I didn't mind being odd man out and everyone knows I'm not woman-minded. But Jules fussed and finally got hold of this Carolyn."

"I know her quite well," I prompted, for he seemed to have melted into silent thought. "She's a pretty child, and rather likable."

"She's a nasty bit of homework! Oh, she looks peachy enough—quite a dish if you happen to be a gourmet. I'm not. She must have put back quite a lot of liquor before she even arrived.

"Then, having acquired an extra female, one of the men cried off, and it all began again. Finally I said I'd get hold of Geoff. Thought it would do him good to eschew expresso. He wasn't too pleased, but I bribed him in my own quiet way."

"It doesn't sound G.'s country. He's practically a teeto-taller."

"There was half Harrods to eat, and G.'s always hungry. Then too, I thought I might offload my sultry partner on him. She was still knocking it back, though she seemed to have a remarkable head. She didn't take much notice of me, and I was just giving up when she said:

" 'Brandon! Funny that! Does your Mother live at Stoke Hempstead?'

" 'She *works* there,' I corrected, 'with a Mr. Grant.'

" 'One way of putting it. At the oldest profession, I suppose.'

" 'What the hell do you mean?'

" 'Oh, don't you know about Ronnie Grant and his secretaries? Such fun! No wonder he pays them well. And their bedrooms are so handy.'

" 'How dare you?'

"She yawned. 'Why not, little Lord Fauntleroy, if it's true? I admit your mother doesn't look the type, but that only shows you never can tell. She's getting on nicely. I'll say that for her. So is our Ronnie. Very slick work indeed.' "

Michael halted, momentarily floundering.

"I'm damned if I like telling you this, Mother, but perhaps you will now see how dreadful the position was. This little bitch was talking at the top of her voice; so was everyone else, fortunately, but I was terrified someone would overhear. But she went on chatting—and drinking. I couldn't stop her. You've no idea what she said about you, and Grant.

"Then, as if things weren't bad enough already, along comes Jules, and typical! puts his foot into it completely.

" 'Make the most of your time, Car! Live it up while you can! It'll soon be nothing but diamonds and mink, bed at nine-thirty and remember your hot-water bottle! Poor little old man's darling, but never mind!'

"They'd known each other since dancing-class days.

"To my absolute horror she began to bawl, really bawl, like Ren when she was a kid. Drunk of course, but howling drunk.

" 'It isn't true,' she kept saying. 'It's *not!* He's nothing to do with me anymore. . . . I wouldn't want him anyhow. I hate him. He and his spare bedfellows.'

" 'Shut up!' I yelled at her. 'Or you'll be sorry.'

"You see how embarrassing it was for me."

"Michael, I wasn't actually thinking of you."

"Well, you can certainly think of yourself. She may be a little tart, but there's no smoke without a fire."

"Need you be so trite?" I asked superciliously. "I happen to be interested in Carolyn, not you or me."

"It must have been about that point when G. walked in, and very high-hat he was.

" 'Gawd Almighty! Who and what are these, Mike? Fugitives from the drinking classes? And look at this little pretty! Vodka, if you please. Leave it to James Bond, poppet. His need is greater than yours—the life he leads.'

"She stared at him. I've never seen anyone stare like that. You'd have thought he was James Bond himself.

" 'Who are you?' she asked.

" 'The man is Geoffrey Brandon.'

" 'Oh.' She wept far more quietly. 'How could I know? How could I possibly know?'

"Meanwhile, I gave G. a hasty, rather garbled resume, remembering with relief his vast experience with the opposite sex. He watched the Linley-Morgan girl while I talked, with a funny expression. Then he just leaned over and took her glass away.

" 'That's enough, sweetie. You don't want to behave like a call girl. You have a Renaissance face.'

" 'G., are you listening? I'm talking of Mother. This is dead serious.'

" 'It certainly is,' he retorted. 'You ought to know better than let the poor child get into this state.'

"He actually blamed *me*. Me!

" 'I'll take her home for you,' he went on. 'Get back to your little friends. Big brother will cope.'

"I went around to see him next morning. He was uncommonly vague. I told him he had to come down to Sussex with me, but he only said I could punch Grant in the jaw on his behalf. More my line than his, he said, and he was late for work."

"He's a good boy, G.," I murmured thoughtfully. "Thank heaven, he turned up when he did!"

"He's insane," Michael corrected. "She's evidently going to be His Next, a nasty little cat like that."

I made no comment. I thought it a pity myself.

I was delivered, like a naughty child, to Falloden Street, where I discovered my aunt bore a strong look of the Cheshire Cat. She ridded me effortlessly of Mike. I don't think I could have endured his company much longer.

"Well, Mitty?" And the face nearly did fade to leave the grin. "Life is full of surprises. Never did I think to see the Brandon boys sally out with sword and pistol to defend their mother's honour. It's as good as a play on Children's Television."

"Nothing funny about it," I replied sulkily.

"We disagree. But Lord, child! What have you been up to? Is it repeatable?"

"It was quite appalling," I said.

"The meeting of Michael and his father? I had a feeling it would come. But why should it be so grisly? They were ostensibly strangers, I suppose?"

"Ronan knew who Michael was. He didn't say anything, but he knew. The boy's the dead spit of his brother."

"Dear me! Rather conclusive, especially if he knew who you were too."

"He found that out just before the end," I said vaguely. It had ceased to be possible to discuss Ronan. "What do you know about all this?"

"Scrappy but intriguing information. Michael rang up to say he was collecting you and would be bringing you here. He was obviously very angry and quite impervious to reason. So I went to Geoffrey's place and ordered him to lunch with me. He was as cool as a cucumber, regretted that he already was booked; and as for you, if you ran around with men like

Mr. Grant, you must expect repercussions. He then added he was lunching with Miss Linley-Morgan and must rush. It was to be passed on, I think."

"She's gone berserk," I said. "Hell hath no fury. G. seems to be calming her down." There was nothing for it but to supply a carefully edited story for her. By concentrating on the split-up between Ronan and Carolyn, I could skate over the thinner ice. I added, of course, a superficial account of Michael's behaviour.

"My only consolation is I'm through with Ronan, and I wish, at this minute, I'd also seen the last of my Brandon boys."

"You need a holiday," my aunt said astringently. "Allow everything to settle and clarify. Lees to the bottom like wine."

"Which ferments," I pointed out, "and explodes if you cork it incorrectly. If it weren't for that, I'd set off for Achna-whinnie tomorrow and damn the whole bunch of them! I heard from Janet Gordon the other day. The croft's going begging."

"Nothing against the place except its name. Far enough away and that's what you need. It would do you good."

With such exhortations and advice, Aunt Trix whiled away the rest of the day, and next morning set off on a visit to Birmingham. My plans progressed in peace and privacy and were already in good trim by the time Geoffrey arrived.

"Your aunt's away for a few days," I said cautiously.

"Bet you're not sorry. I daresay you need a rest after being dragged round the country by the family ape-man."

"So it's your turn to give me a moral lecture?"

"My dear Mum, not my line at all. No, I'm just curious. What did happen at the Moated Grange? A wild youth, my brother, definitely with a St. George-Stroke-Dragon fixation."

153

"He behaved quite abominably. With your sanction, I'm told."

"From all accounts of the diaolgue, I wouldn't back anything so corny. Did you deserve it?"

"You can ask your girlfriend. If I had Mike's outlook, I'd sue her for defamation of character. But I hear you've toned her down a little."

"Lucky for everyone I did."

"Remember you've had a prejudiced account, though I admit the child must have felt like a shuttlecock. She hates my guts."

"Actually she likes you a lot."

"Then she has an odd way of showing it!"

Geoffrey ran his long fingers round the piecrust of an occasional table, and then began to fiddle with a snuffbox. When he spoke, he had a sober air of maturity.

"Supposing I apologized on her behalf, Mum? If you'd rather, she could come herelf, but it might upset her again. She feels very bad about it."

"You don't honestly think I bear her any malice, poor child? She's mixed-up, and if you meet the mother, you'll see why. Don't take it too seriously."

"It's Carolyn I take seriously," he replied slowly. "That's why this is rather important. She doesn't know it yet, but she's going to be your daughter-in-law—God knows when!"

"Just like that, G.?"

"Yes, Mum, just like that."

I was silent, adapting myself to this new, decisive Geoffrey. If only I could dismiss the background muddle, I could feel triumphant. So would another Geoffrey long ago have announced his destiny. I'd always had an itching liking for Carolyn and was surprisingly glad she had fallen into such good hands.

"I've never interfered with you, G., and I'm not going to

start now, but if, as you believe, this is the path of true love, look out. You're not particularly eligible. Have you condescended to tell Carolyn what's in store for her?"

"We both know all we need to know," he replied. "It's enough to go on with. But in view of the circumstances, I thought I'd put you wise."

"Is she your sort of person, G.?"

"I'll see she's no one else's," he retorted. "Mum's blessing?"

"Surely," I said.

It seemed an occasion to supply him with enough money for dinner in romantic surroundings, so Carolyn might be broken in gradually to fish-and-chips.

"You're good value, Mum. It's a fact. Incidentally, what's this Grant chap really like?"

"Quite scrupulous, I should say. Mike flattered him."

"Mike, yes! I *am* going to lecture you, Mum. What are you going to do about him. You'd better get thee to a nunnery, or keep out of St. George's way."

"I just don't understand him."

"He's jealous, that's all. It's one of these interesting psychological manifestations. He'd like to keep you in an ivory tower, never mind how boring and uncomfortable it was, provided you were attached to its front door by the umbilical cord—what a wonderful metaphor! You see, Mum, it's not that you might be a Scarlet Woman that worries him, but rather that you might be a woman at all. Mums are private property. Keep off!"

"He doesn't cling as much as you others. He's rather detached."

"Detached my foot! He's pathologically possessive. I admit that while you're a good girl he's not going to put himself out for you, but step out of line, and you're in trouble. As you've seen. It reminds me of that chap who gave you

155

vegetables. Mike soon booted him out—remember? We're
all fond of you—to a fault—but Ren and I wouldn't force
you into a flat in West Hampstead when you wanted a cot-
tage with roses. You're a person to us, not a cause. And so, I
comfortably believe, are we to you. The odd thing is, you
take it from him."

"In other words, I spoil him."

"Well, don't you? At least, you concentrate on him, which
is the same thing. I tell you straight, Mum, it's got to stop.
Either he learns to control that foul temper of his and live on
the fringe of civilized conduct, or else you must take the
veil, or you'll end up in the *News of the World*."

"I think you exaggerate, G."

"If I do, you still underestimate,' he said.

After he had left me, I thought a lot about him. You took
each child in rotation—surely I'd always been fair? Geoffrey had kept me awake in the past; he would no more. Now
he was ready, even eager, for his own responsibilities. Despite
the problem of Michael, my burden was perceptibly lighter.

Michael! What was to be done about him? Geoffrey was
right, I knew, and that temper was dangerous. I was still
meditating when Pilar came in.

"Another gentleman to see you. A Señor Grant." Too
late to plead I was not at home! It had been too easy after
all!

Ronan walked in slowly. He looked little better than at
our last meeting, but he had himself in hand and it emphasized the vast distance between us. The idea plagued me
that, unfashionable as it was to say so, such men had bought
a sporting chance for the next generation with every asset
they valued. All they gained in return was a bit of ribbon and
vast condescension, whether they lived it out or were engraved on a war memorial. Peace is for those born to its priv-
ileges.

"Do sit down," I said politely.

"Thank you, no. I prefer to stand. I won't keep you very long, but I wish to talk about that boy—Michael, I think you called him."

"Michael James Brandon," I enlarged.

"Brandon? It's a wise child . . . !"

"The converse is equally true."

Metaphorically, I was already backing against the wall.

"I could check on his birthdate, investigate very thoroughly, but is it necessary? He's like Gavin's twin brother. In fact, he's my son."

"*My* son," I corrected. "What can be proved beyond that? My husband never raised any query. Nor anyone else at the time. And now, it doesn't matter."

"It matters to me. I don't like his name."

"Any name at all," I replied, "is better than none."

All the time, I was watching him warily and he measured me in return, calm and insulated. His eyes were cold and hard; the line of his mouth implacable.

"I told you I had only one remaining ambition," he continued. "You knew my heir existed all the time, and you lied to me."

"I said nothing about him."

"Exactly. It puts rather a different complexion on everything, doesn't it? Not an omission one can readily forgive."

For the hundredth time, I tried to weigh up this obsession, founded perhaps as an invalid, fanned by a barren marriage, and brooded over in too much loneliness. Apparently the fact of Michael gave him neither pleasure nor ease.

"You don't deliberately destroy a young person's security," I said. "I've never had any good reason to trust anyone but myself. And had I made an exception of you, was there a satisfactory opening?"

"I think so. Or certainly you could have found the opportunity. However, we now know where we stand at last, and must make the necessary arrangements."

"Are there any that concern you? I brought Michael up; John Brandon gave him a much-needed place in society. Now he belongs to himself. Even if I admit, which I needn't, that he owes his origin to you, it's still irrelevant. These things happen, we know, but no rights are attached to them. I'm neither blaming nor criticizing. I state facts only."

"The boy's mine. It stares you in the face. Something must be done about it."

"It's too late, Ronan. Illegitimacy always is. But here, fortunately, there's no need for Michael to pay the price for our thoughtlessness and self-indulgence. I'm not prepared to accept anything which might disturb the precarious balance of this very successful deception. I would have spared you if I could. But ours was the crime. I intend to keep Michael in the clear."

"You need my consent for that," he replied. "This is rather an unusual situation, a variation of blackmail, where I pay to keep myself quiet. I intend to finance this boy—and you."

"We don't want your money."

"You'll accept it, I think. For if you don't cooperate, I shall be forced to deal with the boy direct. In fact, of course, I hold the key to all sorts of unsavoury information. Your cupboards fairly rattle with skeletons, don't they? It's a pity you weren't more candid; didn't introduce my son to me under less abortive circumstances, so that this could have been done more gracefully. We're now faced with two awkward alternatives. Either you act as my agent, or I do the job myself. Would you like him to be subjected to ordeal by choice? Name versus money? Brandon versus Grant? It would, of course, be necessary to give him a less exaggerated idea of your virtue."

"You wouldn't dare!"

"I might think it necessary. After all, he's going to be a very rich young man, well paid for disillusion. He might think it's worth it. I saw him only for a short time when I was not at my most acute, but I was struck by several things, apart from the disgraceful way he addressed his mother and an older man. First, that such an aggressive and naïve young Puritan could not be expected to take a generous and tolerant view of Brandon history; secondly, well, frankly, he had the aura of the rat-race. I make my living estimating the price of men, and his, at a rough guess, is considerably lower than what I am prepared to pay. One only needs to find the Achilles' heel; I'm sure it's there."

"So you wish to set him apart from the rest of us, make an open exhibition of him? One rich man's bastard! And for all to see! If you'd wanted to lend a hand, you might have thought of it sooner. There was a time when I had little or no pride. You stayed dead and saved yourself a lot of bother. Leave your money to charity, but we don't accept it."

"Don't be a bloody fool, Mitty! How do you think I feel about this!"

"Your conscience is your own business. I'm merely telling you, that if Michael finds out he owes his existence to you and that you left me to battle through for him best way I could, I'm sorry for you. We might even need your precious money to pay counsel for his defense!"

We were both equally angry. Presumably it was the only lubricant which remained to us.

"I'm perfectly aware I've been in the wrong," Ronan's voice was icy and his self-mastery superior, "but I'm suggesting you help me make amends. This young man seems to be at Cambridge. What does he want to do next?"

"*This young man!*" I countered defensively. "You don't think of him as a person at all. You have no right to destroy his security and his peace of mind to satisfy your own vanity.

Keep your money! And keep away from *my* children, who are nothing whatever to do with you."

"Forgive my lack of sentimentality," he said quietly. "But do you really think my one glimpse of my son likely to promote a surge of paternal feeling? You didn't think I'd be proud of him, did you? A young bastard, if I may say so! I only wish to deal fairly with you both. I shall do what I see fit about Michael, without consulting you further."

"Ronan!"

"I'd better go. You chose him, didn't you? Rejected me. Abide by it. You couldn't trust me. If you didn't want me, you might have left me as I was."

"I never want to see you again," I said slowly, painfully.

"You won't," he answered.

His expression was puzzling. I jerked my mind from the obvious parallel, and remembered Mike with all my resolution. Not that I could have touched him. His will, somehow, forbade it. He retreated slightly, and shifted his eyes, as though sidestepping danger. I hated him for it. He needn't be frightened. I wouldn't crawl to him, even for Mike. Let him do what he would—and be sorry for it. My humiliation was just as important as his!

"Did you say you were going?" I asked politely.

He controlled what seemed to be incredulity with an unfamiliar half-smile.

"I must," he said.

CHAPTER 18

In a headlong world, Achnawhinnie had not changed. The croft was a little old house, alone, aloof in its upland valley, guarded by enigmatic hills.

If the pump lay rusted and neglected, if the water now came out of taps, no matter. The place shrugged off progress.

I caught my breath when I found it again, and glad as I was to see them, Angus and Janet Gordon found me absent-minded. After they left me, enough light remained to cross the green and climb toward the foothills of Creag Dubh. The curlews were keening, as curlews will; the sun had already dipped behind the Saddle; and an anxious mother grouse ran from me trailing a wing as she calculated the safe distance between enemy and nestlings.

Evening after evening I kicked the peats and found pictures in the fire. After a hard day's walking over rough ground, worry took second place. The events of the immediate past seemed so improbable it was easier to drift back to the old days when Janet's hair was a red flame and our bairns pushed each other into the burn.

So mental apathy took glorious possession. Everything would sort itself out, given time. Time enough. Time! Nothing to be done. The hills had looked down on far worse human problems. Or on Wednesdays, when the old Laird gave his so-called "tea" parties, I would sit beside Janet, sipping my nonproprietary beverage gingerly, while claymores rusted on the walls, and duelling pistols harked back to real

161

feuds of blood and honour. Later I would walk home feeling life was rather tame nowadays.

My family were always poor correspondents, and apart from Ren's compulsory Sunday regular, Carolyn was the first to write.

Dear Mrs. Brandon,

How right you were! I did meet my match, and through you of all people! I know I behaved dreadfully, but how can I apologize when it brought me Geoff? But I am sorry, really I am. Scared too. I said you were clever and you throw such effective spanners. Could you please stay your hand till you know me better? I'm not bad, truly I'm not, and with Geoff, I could be so much better. Would you hate it very much after all I've said and done? Not that there's any urgency about your reply. Mother, as you can imagine, doesn't like this at all. Anything from seven to ten years' delay will be quite in order.

> Affectionately (*please!*)
> Carolyn

I smiled, scribbled a reassuring reply and tramped down to the Post Office, reflecting that the impatience of youth at least was not one of my problems. Ishbel McQueich was ready for me with a hair-raising tale of local courtship which put mere citified lovers to shame, but thus relaxed, she sent me home with another letter in my pocket—from Michael.

Dear Mother,

First of all, I owe you an apology. I can't imagine why I listened to a type like C.L.M. on the subject of you. I ought to have known better. I've also said my piece to Mr. Grant, so I hope it's the end of the affair.

It was an odd thing. I ran into him accidentally, and he insisted on stopping me to explain the whole muddle. I'd arrived with preconceived ideas, I suppose, which is always a mistake.

He assured me he had no interest in you, or vice versa, and it was most embarrassing for you both. I felt rather a clot. He's not a bad chap really.

Anyhow, the upshot was he asked me to join him at dinner as proof of my repentance, and I don't know quite how it happened —I suppose things were weighing on my mind rather—but I found myself confiding in him about the difficulties of life. I know you think I'm one-track minded, but you don't understand how important this career is to me. Mr. Grant did, for it seems he was once in the same quandary himself. He'd have made a good cross-examiner too! The upshot was he offered to finance me. He makes a hobby of helping young men like myself, having no children of his own. I believe he does it often.

I won't go into details, for I'm enclosing a copy of our agreement which will tell you everything. I've been waiting because, of course, he had to check my credentials and draw up the terms, which are very unexacting really. I have to insure myself and pay interest, but the latter will be postponed till I'm earning enough to cope with it. I know it's not legally binding till I'm twenty-one, but you can't stop me then, and I won't change my mind. You admit yourself you can't afford to subsidize me, so you can hardly object if I make out my own way. It's the perfect solution. I've now got it all taped. Incidentally, a sealed letter for you came with the agreement to be forwarded. I hope it gives extra weight, but if not, my mind's made up.

Sorry about the scrawl,
Michael

It is difficult to accept that a lifetime's training can be erased at one stroke. I had overestimated Michael. For the most superficial glance at the terms of agreement was enough. Under the circumstances, they should never have been countenanced.

Slanting rain needled the windowpanes. I opened the smaller envelope.

Dear Mrs. Brandon,

Your son will have told you the nature of the deal between us, a gentlemen's agreement till he comes of age; after that a straight-forward legal contract.

I would like to help him. Obviously it's impracticable for you to support him till he makes the grade, and his heart seems entirely set on the Bar. Then too, I'm told, you have no strings to pull in what is, after all, a cabalistic profession. I can help here too. He's reported as being an able young man with a good academic brain. An alternative career in business seems undesirable not because he'd fall by the wayside, but rather might succeed too well, too soon. Far wiser surely with his nature to steady and mature him with a background of professional ethics?

I have tried to arrange matters in a way you yourself will find acceptable. In any case, a properly ordered loan could stimulate his sense of responsibility. I add the address of my lawyer. Don't hesitate to communicate with him if you have any queries. You can trust his discretion completely and he handles many such arrangements, so knows the problems, human and otherwise. For the rest, I'm glad to have had the opportunity of helping a promising youngster to the work of his choice. I'm sure he'll do you credit once he has settled down.

I trust you are having a pleasant stay in Scotland and that the weather is treating you kindly.

Sincerely,
Ronan Grant

Thus Ronan won. On terms of compromise perhaps, but he won. He'd offered his apple; it had been eagerly accepted. Odd to think this prim, typewritten summary should be my first and last letter from Ronan! And I would never write to him at all! For there was no conceivable reply. Mike, in his turn, would only read what he wished to see—my consent.

Just one scrawled note to the boy who had failed me when

I most longed to prove him sound. I walked down the glen to post it, as though some hound of heaven pursued me.

About this time I began to fish obsessively, my social enthusiasms were impressive, my minor hobbies innumerable. I scoured the house; I weeded what there was of the garden. I drove myself relentlessly. It wasn't very effective.

The next letter was one of Geoffrey's rare effusions, of uncharacteristic length. After a few dutiful inquiries as to my own progress, he turned to his own tale. It began with Elvira ordering her daughter to take flowers to Ronan Grant, who was on another visit to a hospital. Carolyn's reluctance had enlisted Geoffrey's sympathy. He had carried the bouquet in her place, and learned that Mr. Grant had had a very serious operation and was dangerously ill. So Geoff refrained from telling Carolyn, since she had once had a crush on the man, and gone the next day, this time with a very small bunch of posies and a card with my name! No visitors yet. But the third day he was admitted to the bedroom, on Ronan's orders. The man looked like death and, embarrassed, Geoff had sat silent, sketching, on the pad he always carried, the first thing that came to mind, which was the croft of Achnawhinnie with me at the clothes line. Ronan had come to sufficiently to ask to see the sketch, and learn that Geoff had brought the flowers without my knowledge because I was punctilious about such things. And he was asked to come back, and then again. One time Geoff broke the news about himself and Carolyn, and Ronan—they were on first name terms by then—took it very cheerfully. Exit the wicked Grant.

Now, Geoff went on, Ronan was pronounced as good as new by his surgeon. Ronan maintained it was a miracle and had explained it all carefully to Geoff as though he must understand it clearly. A blow on his head in Germany, Ronan said, had brought on a post-concussional state which, in turn, brought depression and a gradual change in personality. The scar tissue in the damaged area of the brain took years to develop, as a doctor had once predicted, before it reached a stage where surgeons could pinpoint the place by various encephalograms. Surgery had seemed possible, and the removal of the scar tissue relieved the irritation of the brain and the symptoms. Geoff was passing this on because he had a feeling it was what Ronan wished him to do. Now the patient was off to the Bahamas and complete recovery.

There was a P.S. . . . "By the way, I did an undutiful thing, gave away that dishy photograph of you at sweet seventeen. He said it was *bonnie.*"

Like Carthage, I was *delenda.* Everything was clear. I had precipitated Ronan's decision for this operation. I had by my connotations made his plight seem suddenly unbearable. I could guess how it happened, even to date and day. I was so busy with my own need to avoid the future I had not sensed his lack of time ahead. In retrospect every gesture had been indicative of hopeless finality.

Then another miracle—for I believed in them too. The unconscious ill turn transformed into a favour. Now he could make a new start, his debt paid to a self-centered young man. Ronan was free of the past.

So be it. He must be happy now, clear of nagging discomfort and sickness, still young in the world's eyes. He'd meet someone now. Don't let it go wrong. He mustn't be disappointed. And above all, don't let him get ill again! *Please!*

It was raining hard; there was an icy wind. The croft was very cold.

CHAPTER 19

The lambing storms passed and were forgotten. The late highland spring was over and summer came to the hills and the glens.

I stayed on at Achnawhinnie. I managed comfortably. My Pargiton rent was luxury income at the croft, and with Mike off hand and Renata leaving school, I gave up arithmetic.

I paid a brief visit to London at the end of June. What a crowded, noisy place it was! I found myself fretting subconsciously for the evening rise, and my only extravagance, despite Aunt Anglesey's persuasions, was to buy myself a really exquisite new trout rod.

I enjoyed an evening with Geoffrey. He seemed relaxed.

"I want to hear about Achnawhinnie. Also, this is an opportunity to talk about Mike. I'm all for you allowing him to eat his dinners and whatnot—but what is this? The launching's a bit thorough. A trousseau from Savile Row, a man-about-town address, and now a golf club which beggars all description—and its members! Who pays?"

I hadn't envisaged this complication. Ronan had made it part of the bargain that his philanthropy should pass without advertisement, but the trouble was he'd been overgenerous. I decided Geoffrey must have an outline of the case, if only to save him an ulcer. For guidance, I presented it more or less in Mike's own words, hoping it didn't sound too extraordinary.

"Stone the crows!" Geoffrey gasped when I'd finished. "I've heard everything now!"

"Meaning what?"

"Allowing the story is accurate as far as it goes, what does that make my dear brother? It's incredible. The world owes him a wig and gown!"

"He's very young."

"May I quote my Mum and say one is never too young for the ordinary decencies? Allow that Ronan Grant is a Fairy Godfather; allow, to stretch a point, that Mike's so promising he should grasp any opportunity, however mysterious. If my arithmetic were as bad as his, my council houses and cathedrals would fall down. That insurance doesn't begin to cover this sort of loan, and the delayed interest isn't howlingly realistic. Poor chap will be Attorney-General long before he's paid his tailor's bill."

"A slight exaggeration," I stalled.

"I shall go home and drop Ren a line, giving her the approximate cost of flower shops in the West End. The thing is, Mum, if Ronan has this pressing desire to subsidize your children, only your children can stop him.

"I wasn't actually going to tell you this . . . Car said no . . . but maybe I'd better. Ronan—his own choice of name incidentally, no *sirs*, no *Ronnies*—was keen on some modifications to his villa in the Bahamas. Mostly kitchen stuff, which interests me. I rustled up something he could hand over to the local builder, and he wanted to *pay* me. I was annoyed and asked him, why not do the thing properly and charge a guinea a hospital visit? Do you know what he said? 'Because it's far too little, Geoff. There isn't any price at all within my means. I can't even begin to thank you.' And that was that."

"Thank heaven, some one has proper pride," I said.

"A noble youth, your eldest; always was. I went home to

ponder on the psychology of frustrated tycoons. The more I saw of Ronan Grant, the more I wondered about that moated Grange, and was inclined to respect my pretty's loud-boasted intuition, though she's reverted to thinking him the *most* again, and doesn't understand you at all."

"Do either of you ever hear from him?"

"A P.C. now and again to report a Gauguin existence."

"He's making a good recovery?" I was too anxious.

"He didn't say he wasn't." Geoffrey grinned.

I caught only occasional glimpses of Mike who was bidding fair to become a law bore. I gave Aunt Anglesey a modified brief as well, adding that the patron couldn't complain about lack of industry in his protégé. Then I attended Ren's Speech Day and duty was done. Achnawhinnie welcomed me back.

I was disappointed in a way when the holidays came and I was still alone. Ren went with the Lees to Norway; the affluent Michael chose to climb in the Dolomites; while Geoffrey and Carolyn clung to their urban romance. Still, after the twelfth, the village bustled, and there was amusement in watching "coorse Southrons" part with their "siller." It was a measure of my adoption, or poverty, that I was included in the Post Office councils!

Readjustment—but was it really so difficult? My journey through disturbed waters had been of short duration, and aggressive good health is a cure for most ills and broodings. This was my sort of life and I couldn't help enjoying it. It was now inconceivable I should dye my hair blue and become an Anglesey disciple. The decision freed me. I could drift a little longer. If you love the Highlands you do not lightly sacrifice a perfect summer.

I could still be restless, but then I would walk for miles. I remember going over the high tops one day in this sort of mood, and nothing would satisfy me but to come back by

169

the corries of Creag Dubh. It was a dangerous descent; I
hadn't tried it since I was young. I wasn't really surprised
when halfway down my foothold gave beneath me. The
frowning, grey rocks pitched down to a small leaden tarn. It
seemed to move up at me. Vertigo. I don't often have it. I
thought it was the end.

I knew then I didn't mind. My new facade was no more
satisfactory than the old one. I was sorry I was going to em-
barrass my family by dying in an act of dire stupidity, but
that was all the regret I could muster. I was almost disappointed to find myself automatically regaining balance.

CHAPTER 20

I walked home slowly, all virtue gone from the landscape.
In front of me, the croft was a hermit crab's shell; behind
me Creag Dubh was a delusion of strength. As for my beautiful upland valley, it was at best an open prison. I was an
alien, belonging nowhere, and increasingly to no one.

The sun dipped behind the Saddle. It was colder. I must
learn to concentrate diligently on very simple enjoyments—
a hot bath, supper by a newly lit fire, a comfortable bed.
There was a Liederkreis on the Third Programme. I might
fish the moor loch tomorrow. What other diversions? The
list was lengthening, when suddenly my mind emptied. As
I came through the windbreak, ready to cross the burn, there
was a long grey car by the front gate. A Bentley.

A man was sitting on the low stone wall, his eyes on the

sunset. He stood up as I approached. The light was fading; he was part of the half-darkness, much taller, deeply tanned, not like anyone I'd known.

I stopped short of him. I was afraid. He wasn't smiling. Statue-still, he didn't look flesh-and-blood.

The lonely, twilit valley huddled beneath purple crags was a place ghosts could walk, younger ghosts, lovers. Which would mean he had died after all. No Ronan . . . anywhere. Self-denial was only permissible if he were alive and happy within reach of my thoughts.

"Are you real?" I asked. "Please say you're real."

But only the curlews answered.

I had to put out my hand. I didn't want to feel nothing. He took it firmly and laid it against a warm cheek.

"Oh my love!" My voice sounded strange. "I've been wanting you so much."

Had I thought him a ghost? He kissed and kissed me, never speaking, never smiling, never stopping. His hands reclaimed me for his own. His heart beat reassuringly against mine.

"This is where you belong, Mari; close, closer, closest. Can you deny it?"

"Can you doubt it?"

"Oh my very dearest one, I've missed you so much . . . you've no idea how I've missed you. As for doubting, I'd have doubted anything till I saw you again."

"I know."

"But you expected me back, surely? As soon as I was fit enough for this . . . whatever *this* may be! Something very unfamiliar. It must be happiness."

"I think I'm going to cry."

"Go ahead, love. I may join you. I feel most peculiar."

"Don't you dare!" In fact, I began to laugh. "You're so

171

bronzed you'd look silly. You shouldn't have come back, Ronan. You should have found someone else. I wouldn't have minded. I wish you'd beat me. I deserve it."

"I can think of better ways of occupying my time. And, look! Your curls are back again! Aren't you pretty? I always thought so."

Eventually, we went indoors and I installed him by the fire, the light angled so I could see his face.

"As good as new!" I quoted marvelling. "You look years younger . . . nothing like Mr. Grant . . . and quite shockingly attractive. But you're still too thin. Would you like something to eat?"

"No hurry. I've all the time in the world. *Time,* love! Did you hear that? No limit, no tense. A strange luxury, but we're an adaptable pair, you and I; we'll get used to it."

But one didn't immediately. Such wealth was suspect. Explanations, for instance, were difficult to postpone.

"I feel I don't deserve it, Ronan. That quarrel at Falloden Street haunts me."

"I'll soon turn your thoughts into more wholesome channels, idiot! But it was grisly, wasn't it? You looked so lonely, so disappointed in me. But then I was bloody miserable myself."

"I drove you to that operation. I'm convinced I did."

"It's true, yes. Another debt I owe you."

"I could have been with you when the time came."

"The punctilious Mum, hospital-visiting? You were there, love. That little bunch of flowers; that boy's smile! I was very tired, but suddenly I wanted to fight—and did."

"You seemed to like Geoffrey. I'm sorry about Mike."

"Couldn't he be one of the things we postpone? I'm still a bit muddleheaded about him; at the time, of course, I was knocked sideways. A very effective way of curing a morbid parental complex, the sight of a hulk like that! All that the

172

sickly Mr. Grant had ever dreamed of, and yours too! Damn it, Mitty! He even climbs!"

"Oh yes, he's a climber," I agreed bitterly.

"See what I mean, love? You'd better pretend you're a spinster for a wee while. Let's be gay. Undomesticated. We got in a hell of a muddle, and no wonder! But the gamble paid off, and here we are again! Just the two of us. And speaking for myself, quite horribly in love. You wouldn't feel the same, would you?"

Autumn romance! But it happened to be summer. I never heard the skylarks so noisy and defiant, and wherever you looked, harebells drifted, a sea of amethyst. Morning after morning, the sun lit an enchanted world of golden radiance for spellbound wanderers. Night followed sapphire night, ostentatious with stars.

"A sobering degree of perfection," Ronan called it.

"It doesn't seem to sober you."

"I'm happy, *happy*." He smiled. "I feel well; I've climbed a thousand feet today; I'm a man instead of an object. I'd have been content with less. I wanted a lover, I found a companion. And you here in Scotland! And Scotland chose to celebrate my return with its best weather so I could lie with my head on your lap, Creag Dubh above us, the valley below, and feel like a god—or a Scotsman, not that there's much difference!"

We did not go unobserved, but no matter. Those who observed were our friends and approved. Ronan might officially inhabit the local hotel and fish its reaches, but he was more often up the glen.

"Yon's a right bonnie man you have," Ishbel McQueich observed. "An old friend you were saying?"

I had taken to blushing and making rather irrelevant replies.

"He's up here to convalesce from an operation."

173

"Is that so? The late nights are not so good for them, I'm told."

Angus and Janet were more tactful. The Laird had no such qualms. He gave my unfortunate swain a dose of fire-water which nearly brought him to his knees, tripped up his Gaelic in less than two minutes, and finally shouted across at me.

"A suspicion better than y'last, Lassie. Ach, but yon was a dreich wee bit man."

My visit was shorter than usual, and as it was, Ronan complained the road had turned into a dual carriageway.

"I forgot to warn you. He makes it himself."

"I'll recover, gradually. One way of celebrating accept-ance by Achnawhinnie."

"He's wonderful for his age, but he does rather get the wrong end of the crummock."

"Then so do I. I'm glad someone accepts me. This is idyl-lic, Mitty, but high summer doesn't last forever."

"I don't want to come back to earth."

"Not even if I came with you? First we got stuck in the groove of the past, now the present. I'll have to jerk you on, you know, one of these days."

"But not yet . . . ?"

"No, love. I'd better be sober for a job like that. Very sober indeed."

Then one afternoon, it rained. We lit the fire at midday and lounged about. Ronan had brought me up a letter from Ren, which gave me occupation.

"She's at Narvik," I said.

"Is she enjoying herself?"

"I'm not sure. It hasn't the right feel somehow."

"Could be that your sister was mishandling her? Parents are the oddest creatures. They expect the worst so diligen-tly."

"And get it! You needn't be so detached. Look at Michael."

"And look at you now. It's like touching a raw nerve. Funnily enough, I've seen all this before with Gavin and my mother. Can't sleep for worrying. He's a young cub that needs licking into shape—badly. If you ask me, what they all need is a stepfather."

My hands fidgeted in my lap. They were strong and brown; my ring looked fragile, even flimsy.

"I wanted to put this off, Ronan, but I'd better not. You know, don't you, I can't marry you? Such as we have is all we'll get. My first responsibility is to the children, now more than ever. I'm a coward, Ronan, about losing you, but I'd rather choose now than have it forced on me later."

"I see. 'Come let us kiss and part.' How wholesale!"

"Not necessarily. We could still see each other—if you wanted it. We could be discreet."

"Thank you, love."

"Ronan, don't look at me like that! Can't you see how impossible it is? Every instinct screeches warning."

"My instincts tell me that if we play the fool, we'll regret it. We're too old to be illicit. It's damned hard work anyway, and incidentally such news travels fast. Your precious children will discover you in a guilty affair, and then what? Do you forfeit their filial respect, trust to their broadmindedness, or explain how it all came about? Would you like to be proved thoroughly immoral, love?"

"High summer does seem to be over," I sighed.

He took my hand. "It will soon be twenty-five years," he said. "Our secret silver wedding—think of it! We were meant to be so conventional, you and I. My love, hadn't we better remove this bogus ring? You've worn it too long. It gives us a sense of false security. It means exactly nothing to anyone but ourselves. I'm only asking you to ratify this

175

unchanging feeling, to curtsey to the inevitable. You owe it to me, to yourself, even to that boy of ours. I'll climb balconies if you like, or snuggle you to Brighton. You can dictate any damned policy you please, once we're married—but we'll have it written in black-and-white, and the sooner the better."

Instead of waiting for a reply, he kissed me. I could easily have forgotten the subject, but he laughed and pushed me away, smiling quizzically.

"No one need know, I suppose," I said thoughtfully. "We could be like this, just a little longer."

"I thought we might have a honeymoon."

"You can't get married in a minute."

"But at two-thirty on Thursday, love, the minister will spare all the time we need to finish the job."

"You've fixed it all up? With the minister? Oh Ronan, you complacent, single-minded brute! How dare you! I haven't even agreed yet."

"I'll drag you to the altar. By your pretty curls if necessary!"

"Idiot! But I do so love you, Ronan."

"Then supposing you accept me properly."

"I might, if you proposed really elegantly."

"I can't exactly say: *Will you be mine?* Can I? And you know I'm yours, and always will be. What's left? I've actually run out of words, love!"

"And high time too," I said.

CHAPTER 21

Accounts of weddings, for some reason I have never discovered, are abysmally dull unless a pale, sinister figure from the Indies produces a just impediment and the heroine swoons on the altar steps. All of which is exciting, and quite convincing, for was there ever a bride who reached her ceremony believing she would be securely married at the end of it? It's an occupational disease of wedlock. Had you told me as I came through the kirk door on Angus Gordon's arm that Jove was about to strike me with a thunderbolt I would have registered no surprise. What really was astounding, as I walked up the aisle, was to listen to the organ's wheezy assurance that Sheep Might Safely Graze.

I fluttered like a schoolgirl. I lost my sense of humour, even proportion. The Laird in full Highland dress alarmed rather than amused me. I hardly noted Janet's new hat, and when Angus drew my attention to Ishbel McQueich's store of tear-mopping tissues, I frankly shuddered.

"It's a grand turnout," he continued cheerfully and very audibly.

It was. The small, austere kirk was full to bursting point. So much for my quiet wedding! Yet even the strangers from the outlying crofts were more familiar to me than the slim, dark man who waited, unnaturally erect like a subaltern on parade. Beneath his heavy tan, he was pale, and his face held no recognition, no welcome. I wanted to run away, but it was too late.

Ronan Grant. How very odd to be Mrs. Ronan Grant! I
was Mrs. Brandon, Mother's daughter, Aunt Anglesey's
niece. I had three children. I was forty-one.

"Mendelssohn's calling us, Mrs. Grant!" That persuasive, well-remembered voice in my head! "Wake up, love. It's
all over. You've lost a protector and gained a husband."

We proceeded to a Witches' Sabbath. They still talk about
it in Achnawhinnie. Not many southern brides have such a
reception, and few would want one! They dearly love a
birth, death, or marriage in that part of the world, and treat
them all in much the same fashion.

It was a *ceilidh* of formidable proportions, freely under-
written by Ronan's checkbook, and who was I, a woman
of the Sassenach, to judge them? The Laird made a speech
in the Gaelic, which fortunately I could not understand.
Ronan's reply proved he could blush, and speeches safely
over, he shed any trace of Swiss and Lothian blood and his
heart was very highland indeed. The drams bade fair to become gallons. It occurred to me this might go on for days.

"Ye'd best go partner your man in the foursome, or forbye
Ishbel McQueich will be having the breeks off him, and this
his wedding night." The old Laird was at my elbow, his
shrivelled, nutcracker face wreathed with senile enjoyment.

"He shouldn't be dancing reels," I worried.

"Ach, dinna be an auld woman! He's doing fine . . . fine.
An Achnagar Grant if I ever saw one."

The only way to get hold of Ronan, I decided, was to grab
him for a partner.

"Would you be thinking of leaving? Or drinking black
coffee?" But he glided away from me, strathspey time.

"Ronan!" I next gasped in the throes of a complex setting
step. "I don't want to nag but. . . ."

"You are!" He clapped and went away into the reel.

"Darling, you've got to drive. . . ."

"My wife can chauffeur me." He caught me in a Tulloch swing.

I curtsied more unsteadily than he bowed.

"Now, love, what were you saying?"

"You seem to be enjoying yourself," I muttered lamely.

"Ach, and why not? It's a bonnie wedding, isn't it? There never was a better cause to celebrate. Or would you just be looking forward to being alone with me?"

Needless to say, I danced assiduously from that time onwards.

My memories of our honeymoon are tangled. There were such a lot of hotels; the fishing inn, the golfing monstrosity, the struggle for accommodation in the high season. A nice lot of registers for Ronan, who was like a child let out of school, good humour rampant as he retasted the glories of surplus energy. It grew quite difficult to keep up with him—eighteen holes here, a hill climb there, and endless fishing between whiles.

I forget where we hit beams, prints, and chintz and Ronan smiled his crooked, ironic delight.

"When one's young, love's a kind of onslaught," he observed reminiscently. "All right, I suppose, if one doesn't know what it can be like."

"No regrets?"

"Lord no!" He stretched out luxuriously on one of our better beds. "I'd not trade anything for this, would you? Could it be better? Perfection between us, within us, all round us. Let's hope we can keep it a while longer. It doesn't come often, or last long."

"Some people never know it at all." I pondered. "They don't even believe in it."

"Then it serves them right. They don't earn their gratuity. We have, Mrs. Grant—only I didn't reckon on such excessive generosity, an embarrassment of wealth."

The world was well lost, and our old enemy time with it. We had no confines. We wandered; we were pilgrims; we shared a scallop shell of quiet. Had you asked me then why men were born, why women bore them, I should have known the answer. But morning comes to dreamers and they cannot hold their visions.

When we returned to Achnawhinnie, I was absorbed in last-minute chores, while Ronan leafed through the mail with a frown.

"Brandon . . . Brandon . . . and not a Grant among them."

"Were you expecting something?"

"I've had mine. No, I was merely wondering what next?"

"You married a coward, I'm afraid. But you did insist so."

"I think you're wrong, love. Not that it's really my business."

"No, it isn't," I agreed on a note which raised his eyebrows. "I'm sorry, Ronan. I shouldn't have said that, but when I agreed to marry you, it was on the strict understanding that I should use my discretion about this."

"I don't believe in skulking, nor see the reason. I am a perfectly suitable husband, surely, by any standards? I can offer you and your family material benefits. I'm sober—sometimes; industrious always; I'm moderately well connected, have a similar background, and am the appropriate age. Difficult to imagine anyone more eligible. And don't you dare!"

"All true, but it has no bearing on the case."

"*What will the children say?*" he mimicked. "Hell! What can they say? What business is it of theirs? They won't ask you when they come to marry."

"That's not the same thing at all. I'll have to be very tactful and gradual."

"But Michael's the stumbling block—as usual?"

"Ronan, you saw him at Stoke Hempstead. And little or no excuse for a scene like that. G. says he has a *thing* about me."

"It's mutual, isn't it? But since then, he has apologized—and taken my money."

"I'd feel far happier, if he hadn't," I said.

The tension really started when we crossed the border. How right we'd been to stick to the geographical boundary. I began to nurse a dislike of my quandary which gained on me every mile nearer London. The interlude was over.

Ronan decided on the grand gesture, booking us in the biggest suite of the newest hotel. We looked over another, more central, park; there was another balcony, far more austere, higher up into the clouds. Yet you could—and Ronan did—draw sentimental parallels.

"Back in London, my Mari, where it all began."

"But how very different! This suite . . . !" I was feeling better.

"Let's be wild, while we can! Let's buy champagne by the magnum, tip waiters treble. Years ahead to be domestic and staid. We owe ourselves this perhaps. We'll have fun, love. What shall we do? See how high we can run up the dinner bill? Dance the night through? No midnight for Cinderella. Agreed?"

Those downswept enigmatic lashes! Afterwards I was to realize it was his way of ridding me of my hunted look. He smoothed at least six wrinkles off my forehead.

"You can wear that dress you bought in Edinburgh," he added. "Do me credit."

"*I* bought!"

It was a bone of contention between us. True, I had fallen in love with it, but I wouldn't have *bought* it. Shockingly expensive, madly frivolous, it was nothing whatever to do with me. A gown, rather than a garment—elegant, flamboyant, and quite outrageous—it represented, apart from anything else, my customary dress allowance for four or five years. Allowing less need for economy, I still protested vigorously.

"But what do I look like?"

"I daren't tell you, love. You look too young to know."

"Dreadful?"

"I should say *unexpected*."

"I feel superb. Serve you right if I wore it."

And now I would. I'd show him! And come to think of it, I needed something extra for this background!

Accordingly I dressed with supreme care and great amusement. I revealed what I most covered; I ignored plunges into near indecency. Makeup was, of course, essential, and my hair was easily coaxed toward the *outré*. I marvelled at the result. I didn't recognize myself.

Women take mental colouring from appearance. I looked exciting—*me!* I'd led a pretty drab life, but the effects magically disappeared. There was still time to make up for the fun I'd missed.

"A wee bit more shadow, I think." Ronan had materialized behind me. "More mascara too. If a thing's worth doing, do it. You beggar all description, love, and what infinite variety!"

"Are you sure this is feasible? Not that I don't look splendid."

"I shall call you Marietta at last. Only one thing is lacking." I watched his hands in the mirror; they came round my throat almost voluptuously, there to plant a prodigious assortment of enormous diamonds. They winked quite extraordinarily.

"Are they *real?*" I asked naïvely. "Don't they look gorgeous! And don't I look *kept!*"

"Oh, I'll keep you, have no fear of that! I've always wanted a beautiful demi-mondaine. Men are better for a change now and then."

This then was the background, the mood, the characterization. Marietta, status symbol of the affluent; swishing skirts, flashing jewels, practically prancing. A real night out before reverting to sober mother again.

Long before dinner came, I was entranced. I'd never seen him in tails before, a perfect dress for him. Their uncompromising black and white gave me odd spinal tremors. I looked only at him, not at my fellow guests.

At the first we had been tender with each other, overanxious to please, emotionally out of practice. There were ill memories of marriage to disperse, new rhythms to be established. That phase was over. Masculine vanity and female delight in it were now comfortably settled to our mutual pleasure. We were due for a crisis of animal spirits. We could even dismiss our former selves with amused superiority. I don't know how we felt . . . or why. Only that we forgot . . . forgot. . . .

The orchestra was surprisingly "square"—they even played *Always*, and we danced, as we used to long ago, cheek against cheek, in that almost ideal state of eroticism, eternally suspended between the chase and the kill. Ronan murmured the words, changed his mind, and kissed me instead. I didn't care if we were in the middle of the floor.

There is always a remnant of discretion, I suppose, which lurks to impose some conventional limit. Nor was it part of the evening's entertainment to be too submissive. I opened my eyes, straightened my sagging spine, and gazed beyond Ronan's arm.

I found myself facing the glassy stare of my brother-in-law, Arthur Lees.

Now champagne is champagne, and desire is desire, but

the fumes of both can instantly be dispersed by the sight of Peg's husband, not a man to be voluntarily imagined in a mood of enchantment.

The full horror of the situation came to me slowly as though I had not the strength to absorb it in one glance. I took a deep breath. Peg in sequin-embroidered morocaine, Aunt Anglesey favouring rich purple velvet. Renata was wearing Ronan's stars, Carolyn blazed warm in crimson. Geoffrey next. Then Michael!

With one trembling shudder I returned to sanity.

"Ronan! Something quite shocking has happened. What shall I do? They're *here* . . . all my family . . . even Peg and Arthur. They've seen us."

He continued to waltz calmly, though he gradually slewed in their direction. I had a hysterical impulse to hide him, spirit him away.

Aunt Trix had only half her grin, Peg's mouth was slightly open, Ren's telltale skin spread a blush to the roots of her hair. There was a lost, bewildered air about her. Geoffrey was different, older. He lit a cigarette which in itself was significant; his hand shook. Michael again, and it was he who really held my attention. He was so pale, his contracted brows were satanic, and a muscle twitched unguardedly in his cheek. His features had sharpened; his mouth was a ruled line.

"I can't cope. Not tonight, Ronan. Get me out of here. Oh, why did it have to happen like this?"

"Pull yourself together, Mitty." It was obvious he had. "The end of our honeymoon but not of the world. I don't believe in running away. Try and smile, and we'll get it over."

He had become a managing director facing difficult shareholders. He propelled me coolly to their table.

"What a pleasant surprise," he drawled. "Heaps of Brandons and suchlike. Mrs. Anglesey! What a long time since we met! And Carolyn—you look most alluring, but then you always do."

War into the enemy camp, a good aggressor with a poor second-in-command. I mumbled the balance of introductions. The Lees were disposed of adroitly. He turned to Renata.

"We've never met," he smiled, "but I've heard a great deal about you." He put out his hand. She left it alone, her colour deepening if possible. I could see she was nearly in tears.

We must have attracted attention, so it was as well Carolyn saved us total social shame. She had been glancing round my trio warily, now she took a plunge into the awkward silence.

"We were just talking about you, Mrs. Brandon, and wishing you were with us. Then we looked up, and there you were! Or someone very like you! You look quite fabulous. As for Ronnie, I mistook him for the Brazilian ambassador."

I still looked sideways at the boys. In their trim dinner jackets, they were disconcertingly like tailors' dummies. Not an ounce of colour in either face. Geoffrey lit another cigarette. His average was one a year at Christmas.

"Ren and her aunt and uncle," Carolyn continued valiantly, "are just back from Norway. Aunt Trix thought they ought to see Life as lived down South. And of course this place is the *most*. I promised Mother I'd look out for film stars, and thought momentarily Mrs. Brandon was the latest importation from Italy."

"I'd use another word," Michael interrupted viciously.

Ronan's grip tightened on my arm, then he deliberately let me go as though to free his hands.

Aunt Anglesey intercepted. She addressed the world in general.

"Not surprising you've all forgotten what Mitty's like. It's so long since we've seen you, child. Besides, you look more like a resident than a visitor." She was the only one of them who could price my necklace at sight.

It was a hostile opening but I braced myself to take it. Unfortunately, I hesitated and missed my cue. Michael's control was slipping.

"I warned you," he addressed Ronan directly. "How dare you encourage my mother to make an exhibition of herself? A woman of her age."

"It's you who are making an exhibition of yourself, Michael. In a public place." Ronan was dangerously quiet.

But the boy was out of hand. "Oh, I'll deal with you privately, never fear. No man lies to me and gets away with it. And from now on, leave my mother alone."

"Michael," I tried to interrupt.

"As for you, the others can take you away while I settle with Grant once and for all. And perhaps you'll think twice before you shame us again. You look like a rehabilitated call girl."

"What did you say?" Ronan almost anticipated my gasp. "How dare you speak like that to my wife! Take a grip on yourself and stop threatening me. I, and only I, shall be taking your mother away until her children are capable of elementary courtesy. We're in Suite Five if anyone wishes to congratulate us."

"It's true," I sighed, and wished it were not.

Ronan turned to the others. "I'm exceedingly sorry to be so abrupt, but I didn't start this scene. This young man has no idea how to conduct himself, so I'd better remove the cause of irritation. We only reached London late today. Mitty intended to get in touch with you tomorrow, and as things stand, had better keep to her schedule. She's tired and understandably upset. I now see plainly why she postponed any formal announcement."

Their speechless amazement was not very flattering. You'd have thought they might have guessed what was coming, even though the timing could scarcely have been worse. Michael had frozen. Ren had a curious rigidity. Geoffrey looked ill. Carolyn who had been eyeing him anxiously was the first to recover.

"But what fun!" A redoubtable girl. "So I was right all the time. Didn't I say so, Geoff? Now perhaps folk will respect my intuition. I hope you'll both be wildly happy. I've often wondered what Ronnie really meant to me; now I see precisely. He's my ideal stepfather-in-law."

Ronan could still smile. "I'll look forward to that, Car. And thank you."

Aunt Anglesey rose majestically and delivered a brief peck on my cheek. "Wish you luck, child, sly puss that you are. I must hear all about everything tomorrow. For I must say this is the oddest outing I've ever had. And meanwhile I agree you look wretched, the effect being heightened by that strange black stuff round your eyes. My nephew-in-law would be wise to give you a brandy and put you to bed without further ado. You may come and see me in the morning."

It was not, in the circumstances, a helpful or tactful speech. I scarcely noticed the more gracious comments of Peg and Arthur. Ronan fidgeted with impatience, the children were silent and stony.

Honeymoons don't last forever.

CHAPTER 22

I stared straight ahead of me, numb with misery. From time to time, tears would gather, never to disperse. The milk was spilt; no point in crying.

"I've failed them," I said at last. "I've failed them completely."

I wouldn't let him put his arm round me. I kept pushing it away. "Leave me alone! You made me break my promise . . . let them down . . . for what? Self-indulgence . . . repaired vanity . . . the taste of youth lost years ago."

"For a degree of loving that's completely beyond them."

"Don't you mean sex?"

"They failed you at the test, after all you've done for them. Selfish, inconsiderate, cruel—and that goes for your damned aunt too! If that's the best your family can do, even I am an improvement. Whatever they felt, they could have behaved like civilized people. If they can't see you have a right to your own life, they're not worth this heartbreak, not worth it. God knows you've had your share of the rough! How dare they begrudge you the smooth!"

"They've never seen me really happy. I was tonight. I suppose I looked stupid. I'd forgotten, Ronan; I *felt* young; I wasn't just playacting. They had to wait till now to interpret me for once. No wonder they were ashamed!"

"Poor love! Don't be absurd! You're nothing to be ashamed of. I'm proud of you—think of that! Of myself too for learning exactly what you are, with a damned sight less opportunity than people who've lived with you for years. I'm a man of taste, my love, and discrimination. It gives me satisfaction when every mature man looks at you with pleasure, and most of the women with open envy. You're just the type to acquire a second husband, children or not. Wouldn't you rather have me than anyone else?"

I was deaf to his cajolery. "Not as things stand," I said.

"Oh come now, love. You've hit lucky at last. I am prepared to *give* sometimes, not just take and take."

"You don't understand, Ronan. You see me so differently, the eye of love. A sort of astigmatism. To them, I'm old, worn-out, pathetic."

"We've neither of us reached forty-five yet. You talk as though we were ninety when we can't even add it up between us. And hell! What if we were a hundred? You'd still be my black-out girl, my grail from the junkshop. I was there before when everyone failed you; I'm still around for when things go badly wrong. Continuity, you see! I always did enjoy looking after you. It's what I'm here for."

"Ronan, I've never said this even to myself. I do realize I wouldn't have come through that blitz without your help. I was too mad and muddled. I did wrong, and I've never caught up with the accumulations of error. Mike's like a millstone round my neck. I can never bury Johnny. And my punishment is apt. They're entitled to stand between me and my peace."

"You wouldn't listen if I argued. Just the same, at worst, I share irresponsibility equally. The reprisals are mine too. Ach, but it's nonsense! You did the right thing for all of us, at a terrible cost to yourself. As for Michael, yes. But I suggest you transfer that weight on me. You'll probably have to anyway."

"Did you see Geoffrey's face? It took time to see what was wrong with him. I knew I had to keep you and the children apart. I *knew* it."

"What do you mean? Geoff behaved oddly certainly."

"He's a portrait-painter *manqué* with a subtle eye for a likeness and a love of detail. I suppose it was seeing you side by side. You've filled out, Mike's fined down, and you have the same tricks when you're angry."

"Mitty, he's a kind lad and genuinely fond of you. This is bound to shake him, yes, but give him the chance to recover. I'm damned if we need excuse ourselves. Let him face the test. You may find he's able to shift the blame onto me, which would be much easier for us all."

"Why should they misjudge you?"

"My back's broad, and I'm not emotionally involved beyond a slight itch to murder that young lout of mine. Let them be critical and censorious. We paid for their pretty status in advance. That they have illusions to lose is an achievement in itself."

I looked at him then. He was tired, he'd lost colour, there was an anxious frown between his eyes. Poor Ronan, learning the joys of family life a little too quickly! There was a lot in what he said. Must we always consider the young at the expense of our own, more companionable generation?

He smiled at me, guessing perhaps how my mind was working.

"I still shouldn't have married you."

"I browbeat you, love. Blame me. But Mari, I did need you; more than you'll ever know. I think we did right too. And not just because we love each other—and they've had a more than generous share of you to date—but darling, I belong in this coil as well. You need my help if we're ever going to get in the clear."

"I'm not exactly saying we're in the wrong. Only that we should have waited till the children were off hand."

"Christ! Haven't we waited long enough, nobility and all —and look where it's landed us! Stop thinking of them. Stop it! How the hell do you think I feel, facing up to the truth that those stupid, ignorant young fools must always mean more to you than I do? All right! You regret you married me. I don't blame you. For having done so, you took on more duties. I'm your husband, not your lover. You're supposed to cleave only unto me. I'm not demanding you forsake all others, merely that you don't forsake me. I've never asked you to choose the better or the worse, but if they force the issue, they'll damned well get what's coming to them—and so will you! I'll win to my own satisfaction, Mitty, and you know it. I'm sick and tired of your children, your first husband, brothers, sisters, aunts, the lot! I took you right from under their insensitive noses and legally secured you for good and all. I never was a defensive fighter. I'm no good at rearguard action; they're welcome to it. Meanwhile, I'm in possession, and intend to make good use of both rights and opportunities."

He'd never made love to me in anger before. I didn't know I was a primitive woman. Curious our interrupted playtime should end in a new brand of ecstasy.

Despite the new complications, we kept to our planned schedule next day. Ronan went off to his board meeting. I went along to Falloden Street, and found my aunt in her office.

"Well, Mitty. Are you satisfied? Wounded vanity healed. And hell to pay."

"Of all the unlucky things! That the whole tribe of you should collect in such an unlikely place!"

"My good Mama," her grin was more in evidence this

191

morning, "brought me up to behave at all times as though great Jehovah, all his minions, and my entire family, were inspecting me through field glasses like celestial ornithologists."

"I hope they found nothing amiss," I snapped. Stress was not improving my temper.

"I was never caught out, child, which is the operative point."

"I see I'm under your grave displeasure. Disappointing when you're the only person knowing enough to show fairness."

"I'm not surprised, of course. You intended to get that man at any cost, despite your protestations to the contrary. So much for your concern for your children. All talk! If you can't consider them, you don't deserve them. Aren't they worth a compromise?"

"Is there any point in this sort of discussion?"

"Probably not. The children, as you saw, are all completely shattered. No doubt you've also omitted to inform your mother."

"I told no one at all," I said. "And thank heaven I had that much sense, so I could enjoy a modest allotment of the companionship everyone grudges me. Why should I ask permission to marry again? I think you're all mad."

"Is he pleased with his heir? I saw little evidence of gratified parenthood."

"My greatest regret is that I ever confided in you. You need never have known about Michael, or his father. Or John and Martin. You might have helped with the children, honestly wished me well, in an apparently unexceptionable marriage. But I, like a fool, fell for the luxury of confession."

"If you hadn't, you'd still be Mitty Brandon."

On this note, I continued upstairs to tackle Renata. I found her fidgeting with some ornamental grasses, a study of exaggerated unconcern. Her eyes were swollen, and she kept them averted.

"I wondered if you'd come." She spoke jerkily.

"Are Arthur and Peg still about?"

"They're off this afternoon."

"Oughtn't you to be with them till they go? Politeness?" She spun round to face me.

"Do you think after last night I'd go near them? They'll be discussing you, chewing you over, wondering what that man's *worth*. As if it matters. I could have died . . . *died!* I was so ashamed. It was horrible enough in that awful hotel with the boys looking green at the gills. But afterwards it was worse. . . . Uncle Arthur said you knew which side your bread was buttered. . . ."

"I wonder if you could accept that I'm very fond of Ronan, or am I beyond the age of affection?"

"We were all right as we were. Nothing will ever be the same again."

"Nonsense."

"It isn't. You've changed already. I didn't recognize you last night. You weren't like my Mother. And you've cut off your hair. I don't want you to look younger," she sobbed. "You looked comfortable and safe before."

"I can't do right, can I? Listen, Ren. Do you know I've never worn my star pendant with an evening dress? In over twenty years I've never had a night out, dancing, laughing, having your famous *fun.* I wanted to. Just once. Can you understand that?"

"I don't mind you dancing, if that's what you want, though it seems queer at your time of life. But you didn't have to marry him. Why did you?"

"You don't want me to say I fell in love with him, do you?"

"Be your age! I expect the truth is you went soft because he was always being ill. I expect you agonized over him like you did when we were ill. Then you began to think it could be a sort of job for you when you were older, and in the country, too."

"Even at my age," I laughed, "I'd be ashamed to admit to such pedestrian emotions."

"Oh, Mum, I feel beastly. And I've said such dreadful things. I didn't mean them. But what shall we do without you?"

"You'll be seeing me more, not less."

"What's the use, if he's there? Oh, I see what you see in him, but I wish it wasn't you, if you get what I mean."

"You must be recovering. Your usual syntax is returning."

She began to hug me. "Oh, Mum, I will try and like him just for your sake. And I'll help you buy dishy clothes that really suit you. You're not adventurous enough. But Mike's rampaging. Don't let him upset you. He never thinks of anyone but himself. I suppose I really ought to see Aunt Peg off."

I decided it wasn't a bad morning's work, Anglesey or not, and was sorry Ronan was lunching in the city. At the hotel Carolyn was waiting.

"Glad I caught you," she said, "between bouts of brats. Could you stand me lunch?"

"If you can bear with someone of my age."

"Supposing I called you Mitty and treated you as a contemporary? You were gorgeous last night. As for Ronnie, he's absolutely bedazzled. Am I responsible for any of this? Mind you, Geoff always said there'd be trouble if you ever got yourself a man. Mike and so on. But why isn't Geoff pleased? He wanted you settled. He knew perfectly well Ronnie was in love with you. Yet now he won't even talk to me about it. And he's fabulously tolerant and damned fond of you, too."

I hedged. "Was I very outrageous last night, Car? What was the reaction of an impartial judge?"

"I'm not impartial. It made me feel secure. I've always felt youth is very short for a woman. She must hurry and grasp. It was my father, I suppose. I was fond of him. He went off with that young girl. It was like a warning. As if it must happen to me too. It didn't seem much of a prospect, until last night. I couldn't take my eyes off you two. You seemed to shriek that it was to do with people, and age didn't come into it. You've found what I need."

"You sound like Ronan. But you're both in the minority. What I don't understand is the nature of this sex blind spot. I keep thinking of my mother in her forties. Disarmingly pretty . . . delicious hats. . . . Father indefatigably appreciative. Nobody worried. We took it for granted. Sad that the more you give, the more's expected of you, but that's how it is. Neglect your children, Car. It's fair advice."

As soon as lunch was over, I squared my shoulders and took a taxi for Geoffrey's flat, alerted for trouble, and determined not to buy my future at anyone's expense.

Geoffrey greeted me courteously but remotely.

"I'm not going to do this well, I know," I began. "Ren and Aunt Trix have already spoken their minds. It might be simpler if you poured fourth invective and got it over."

"I can't think of any at the moment. I behaved badly last night. No excuse."

"There were extenuating circumstances."

"None the less, I'll never win a good conduct medal that way. Is it too late to hope you'll be very happy? Ronan Grant seems a nice chap."

I wonder what it cost him? I'd never liked him better. I suppose my expression reflected something of my sympathy. He didn't want it.

"Actually," he added, "I drank too much last night. One shouldn't. Have you ever had double vision?"

"Sometimes," I said slowly.

"I suppose you get used to it, given time."

"Yes."

"I was fond of my father."

I nodded dumbly.

"It makes sense at last," he continued. "Doctors always maintain the alcoholic is someone who's failed and gone under."

"I'd hoped you were too young." I was jerked into trailing speech.

"One stores that sort of information till one can explain it. Maybe I had to wait till I first went on a blind myself, and knew suddenly I daren't beat it up like the others. I knew too, there was something wrong between you and my father. I wish it could have been left at that."

"Would it help, G., if I told you John never knew? I wasn't responsible for his drinking. The war did that for him. In peace, we are surrounded by people without knowing how their natures stand up to stress. It was active service, not me, which tipped the scales. In a different world altogether, your father might have made good. Regular domestic life might have helped him, too, early on, but we had no home and saw very little of each other. I did love him when I married him, but he changed."

"I'm glad he didn't realize . . . about Mike."

"Ronan was very good to me, and facing a suicide mission besides. I knew I was doing wrong; but wrong had lost meaning. When he came back after all, he ceded his rights, never told me. And I only tried to do my best for all of you, even John."

I stood up and pulled on my gloves. "I'm sorry to burden you with these confidences, G. You've been a good son. And as for your father, I know he was unhappy, but I'd have given much to have had it otherwise. I did what I could. I stuck to him. We were unlucky. You needn't be. Marriage is a gamble, but usually worth it."

He took my hand and pulled me down again.

"Don't misunderstand me, Mum. I *was* fond of Father, but you . . . well, you're *you*. I'm vaguely shocked. All these men in your life, and you had to battle for us alone. I'm surprised at Ronan! I don't want to know about it . . . it's all too obvious you must have been deadly serious. But I can't help wishing, weakly, it could have taken place earlier when we were too young to ask questions. It would have been more comfortable for me—and infinitely better for Mike."

"Mike!" I said. "I might have known you'd behave well under any impossible circumstances, just as he wouldn't."

"How's Ren?"

"Getting used to the idea. Better than Aunt Anglesey."

"Well, her fish got away, didn't it? She'll be dressing Lavinia in black brocade yet. No; I fancy, Ronan himself's the trouble. Not the type to stand for nonsense. I wouldn't dream of crossing him myself."

"Mike will surely leave well alone?"

"You never know what Mike will do," Geoffrey said.

Back at the hotel, I found Ronan working apparently in carefree comfort on a pile of business papers. I poured out the events of my day. He listened attentively and with few interruptions.

"Which leaves Mike," I concluded. "I must go and see him this evening."

"You won't find him. He's cleared out, having returned every penny borrowed and ripped up our agreement. I haven't seen him. The envelope came when I was in the meeting. We can now nourish a frail hope he may keep out of the way till he's simmered down."

"But where's he gone?"

"I haven't the least idea, love."

"But I must see him . . . explain. . . ."

"What, for instance?"

I shrugged wearily. "I'd have thought of something. And having misjudged G. and Ren, I'm probably wrong about Mike too. Did you say *all* the money? How, I wonder?"

"Mari, relax. What about a drink and a good dinner and a spot of oblivion? The situation has improved since yesterday; rejoice and leave well alone."

"I'm not having dinner in this place again."

"We'll find a check tablecloth in Soho and we'll discuss relativity instead of relations. Would you enjoy a show?"

"Indeed no. I've had enough drama for one day."

There was a tailpiece. When we got back a note waited for me in my aunt's characteristic scrawl.

Dear Mitty,

You have doubtless worries enough so I'll spare you one. Michael asked me for money which I understand was to repay his debt to your husband. I thought it might help him to feel free of obligation, and prevent him from borrowing elsewhere. He was very quiet, refused tea, and didn't see Renata. After a spell of his company, I did not feel optimistic about his talents as a stepson. He promised, however, to send me his address when he resettled.

Renata was happier after your visit. We had a long chat and she was far more cooperative. She quite understands the disadvantages of playing gooseberry during your settling-in period, and Peg, bless her! will look after the child in a week or two. Meanwhile she goes to Lucy, well out of the way. Later, when I'm less busy, she can come back here, and we can arrange a few preliminary outings *carré* so she can adjust to your husband painlessly and gradually. By this method, everyone will be pleased. . . .

Your affectionate aunt,

Beatrix Anglesey

"Good God!" Ronan read the letter over my shoulder. "I'm not pleased for one."

"About Michael? I'm most relieved."

"No, not Michael. That unfortunate little girl."

"She'll be better with Peg, even Mother."

"You're not serious, Mitty? Didn't you say she was miserable? And couldn't she be seeing too much of your sister and that dreich man? Besides, this is surely the best way of alienating her from us beyond hope of repair. She should be getting to know me. I don't mind having her at the Grange. I expected it."

I smiled patronizingly. "You don't know what she's like ordinarily. Not restful. This plan is much better. It will give her time to cheer up, and a breathing space for us all. You see, they all agree."

"And if I said I wanted her with us?"

"Well, Ronan, I do reserve the right to use my discretion about my own children."

He narrowed his eyes and looked at me speculatively.

"I can take a snub as well the next man," he replied lightly.

CHAPTER 23

Renata and I went shopping next morning. She was anxiously friendly but distrait. At lunch she discussed her approaching tour of relatives with calm if not enthusiasm, and filial duty thus done, refused my invitation to a West End cinema and slipped away from me. I was left with a sense of alarm. I had become an ordeal. My children would increasingly avoid me, rather than make the uncomfortable effort. Nor could I blame them.

I was grateful for a quiet afternoon. I'd told Ronan I wouldn't be back till late and he intended to catch up with office work. I left it at that, took off my new town clothes and slipped under the eiderdown. It was wonderful to be alone and peaceful, and hours of it ahead.

I've no idea how long I slept. Then I was alert at once, concentrating fearfully. Not that the two naturally clear speakers in the adjacent room took any trouble to modify their voices My uncancelled note would still be lying for all to see. They had every reason to think me streets away.

"I warned you. This is it. You've had your dirty money back. Did you think you could bribe as well as lie to me?"

"Yes," Ronan's voice was scornful. "And I was very successful too."

I struggled into a dressing gown and went over to the door. It was just open. I couldn't see them, but I could hear every word. I was afraid interruption might precipitate an even more dangerous situation.

"To think you bought me off! Do you imagine I'd owe my career to you?" Mike was saying furiously.

"I was a little surprised you should, I confess, and that it should be so easy to make a fool of you. A little more opposition would have been gratifying and stimulating."

"You're clever, aren't you? Keep me quiet at the operative time so you can have a free hand with my mother."

"No, I was ill. There was plenty of time for you to go up to Scotland and justify your conduct. Or later. No one stopped you from visiting Achnawhinnie. You neglect your mother, Michael. Face it."

"So now you have the effrontery to tell me how I ought to behave?"

"Stop shouting, Michael! You may think I'm senile, but I'm not deaf! I would imagine it beyond most people's scope to teach you civilized conduct. I'm merely criticizing you. And I also wish to know what this is all about. I courted your mother quite openly and conventionally. I'm now living, not in sin, but in an honorable estate. I add no more, as you seem to me the sort of young man who is incapable of understanding more complex explanations."

"You tricked her into it. You misled her, probably lied to her as you did to me."

"Don't talk such bloody nonsense! My wife loves me and I love her."

"Love!" The word seemed to hold a special, obscene horror for him. "Don't make me laugh! To think of that sort of thing in connection with one's own mother is beyond everything. And to marry again! She used to say she never would . . . she didn't want to . . . she promised."

"Let's get this straight. You think, after all she's done for you, she should reject a chance of happiness and security, to please a spoiled boy who's pathologically jealous?"

"Happiness! Security! I remember what it was like. I was only a child then . . . helpless. It was dreadful. When the miracle happened and he got killed, just the way I'd always prayed he would, I saw to it that no other man ever hung around her. Until you came along I was equal to them. Now I've let her down."

"Interesting!" How could Ronan sound so cool, so mocking? "What do you anticipate? That I put Mitty through ordeal by fire? Or is this just stepfather trouble? I should have thought John Brandon had been dead long enough to have his place usurped, and his obituaries filed away. Besides, you don't sound particularly fond of him."

"Fond of him! So now I'm supposed to be in mourning for him? I hated him. I'd have killed him myself if I could.

I'd lie in bed at night, thinking out ways, dreaming I were older, bigger, stronger. And not afraid, and helpless and little anymore. I once had a nightmare . . . got up the way kids do to run to Mother. But they were down in the hall. He was shouting, shouting at her. He looked distorted, terrifying. I saw him hit her . . . hit my mother. In a few minutes there was blood . . . all over her face . . . everywhere. She sort of whimpered. I couldn't bear it. I couldn't help her."

I knew exactly when it must have happened. Mike would have been five perhaps. It was all the more shocking because it was an isolated occasion. Johnny wasn't usually aggressive, my nose didn't usually bleed. But he could be noisy and I'd try to quieten him. To think that frightened eyes peered down the dark stairway; that the rogue event can cast so long and hideous a shadow. We try so hard; we mean so well; we fail so bitterly!

Michael's voice went on, expressionless now, hypnotized by memory. "Every night I'd lie awake waiting for him to come home. I'd hear him fumble with his door key and I'd begin to tremble all over. I'd wait for the shouting with my head under the bedclothes, but the silence was nearly as bad. I'd feel sick. I didn't tell her. I couldn't help her and I was afraid she would cry. I couldn't bear to see her cry . . . ever."

Ronan seemed to be speaking to someone much younger. He was patient but astringent. "Ought we to be talking like this? Ought you to have told me that story? You must respect your mother's reticence, Michael. She had a bad time. I can see this is a difficult ghost to lay, but you must try for her sake. As for me, I shall never harm her. Make sure you don't either."

It wasn't, I thought, a very sympathetic speech, not that it mattered. The boy was impervious to tact or reason. I wondered, indeed, if he heard, caught up as he was in a web of misery and protest.

"I believed she was safe now." He sounded incredulous. "I thought she was too old."

"Can't you understand mutual dignity between the sexes at all?" Ronan inquired curiously. "One of these days, you'll marry too."

"Never! Leave sex to those who like it!"

Ronan couldn't have been far away from me for I heard him swear under his breath. Well, it was a bitter moment. The child I'd given him was proved an emotional cripple, not because of his irregular birth, but due to my own subsequent stupidity and lack of vision. And then another thought came, even worse. Was I really to blame, or was this the old evil still destroying? Hadn't Aunt Anglesey seen in Michael a suspicion of Martin? Might I not have ignored what I hated too much to recognize?

"Well, that explains a lot," Ronan said quietly. "You don't like sex; nor love, nor marriage. But you're odd man out, and you can't expect them to disappear from the world at your command, Michael. The average man and woman need physical reassurance deeply, and it's their greatest privilege to give it to each other, and at the same time extend understanding and companionship. Your mother and I are fortunate. We even have that rare bonus payment, the link with immortality."

"If you knew, only knew, what a fool you sound! You and mother! Who's going to listen to you?"

"You are, Michael. For I'm deeply shocked, that a young man of your age hasn't more sense. I do not choose to have my feelings toward your mother diminished and ridiculed by a half-witted boy. As for my age, at least I have this advantage over you, I do enjoy normal reactions. And always did. As you despise middle-aged emotions, you'd be happier perhaps to know I wasn't much older than you when I first met your mother, and she was only nineteen. It wasn't just that she was the loveliest thing I'd ever seen, that looking at her I found everything worthwhile in life, I knew the first moment that all peace must shrink into the one boundary; then, now, always. It was suddenly worth being born in a difficult world; it was easier to die for causes otherwise inexplicable; and meanwhile life had a new dimension.

"You worry about my marrying her. Long before you were born, she was mine. I staked my claim, but it's taken a long, wasted time to realize it. Now she's my wife. No one can take her away from me. Of course, when we first met, she was married to Brandon, whom she stuck to for the sake of your brother who was only a baby at the time. It wasn't as if I had any alternative to offer. We thought I had only a few weeks to live. She was a generous, brave child. Her future would have been smoother had she been less so. What sticks in my gullet is that her sacrifice and courage should be sneered at—and by you of all people! It's absurdly ironic that you, my dear Michael, should be the one to try and cancel that love and loyalty. I'm grateful I was born into a generation which, for all its hazards, at least allowed destructive instincts to be suitably canalized. Do you realize I bought your kind the freedom to be irresponsible, spineless, and cruel? But I'm still here; still coping with your sort of person. Leave my wife alone. She's worth six of you."

"How very touching! The grand war love story! Quite Hollywood. Three-and-sixpence worth of technicolor frustration for the back stalls."

"Did I say *frustration?* Surely not. Desperation, yes. Compensation, perhaps. Perils are paid with pleasures. I remember saying so. I may have been going to the wars, but I didn't love honour more. Not more than I loved her. And beds, you know, had already been invented."

I leaned against the doorjamb. The sharp change of tone hit me as it must have hit Michael. The end of the fuse. I waited numbly for the explosion.

Michael spoke very slowly after a long silence. "Now you're talking, so let's use the straightforward words. You made her an adulteress, didn't you? No wonder her husband beat her up. So you're the cause! Why blame my father? Unfaithfulness is an excuse for worse outrages. She deserved all she got, maybe more, leaving her children to go off with some strange man."

I think I went in automatically. I was on scene, but invisible.

Michael was the burlier of the two men. He was not playing with anger; it possessed him wholly.

By comparison, Ronan was relaxed. I have seen cats flex their bodies in just that way. His arms were hanging loosely, he moved his feet slightly into a bracing position. Wary and attentive, he waited for his cue, his eyes cold and calculating.

"I must remind you," his voice cut like steel, "that I'm twice your age and have a bad record of health."

"You don't get out of it that way, you. . . ."

Ronan flicked in almost before the obscenities.

"And it's not customary for a son to strike his own father."

Michael hurtled forward blindly, ready to choke, to throttle, to kill. Ronan was smiling! I'd never seen danger personified before. So this was Captain Grant at zero hour! He waited ice-chill, almost amused. Beautifully and implacably, he led with his left and cross-hooked with his right. Down went his victim, sprawling, prone.

I was over to him in a flash. "What have you done? He hit his head. He's bleeding. What have you done to him?"

"Where on earth did you spring from? Stop talking rubbish, Mitty, and pull yourself together."

"You intended to do this. You baited him. You knew he
had this dreadful temper. How dare you destroy my work of
years? How dare you betray me? And if you were determined
to kill my poor Mike, you might have let him die with his illusions."

"Oh shut up!" he said. "I want to think."

"I watched you. You meant to do this."

"Naturally," he snapped. "Do you think I could stand
up to a hulk like that for ten rounds, Queensbury rules?
He's merely stone-cold, and you'd better get to hell out of
here before he comes round. I don't think he'd enjoy your
witnessing his downfall. You were brought up with brothers. Have some sense. You seem to have made a pretty good
mess of this boy, the least you can do now is avoid any more
damage."

He pushed me unceremoniously out of the way and ran
his fingers expertly round the carcase.

"No bones broken. Good news for a loving mother. All
right, you lout! Come to!—Mitty, are you going of your own
accord, or do I have to lock you in the bedroom?"

If I obeyed, it was because I couldn't face Michael. It was
enough to hear his voice again, interrupted by Ronan, lazy,
mocking, under perfect control.

"So you've had enough? Good! Because I've had just about
enough of you, Michael. We've heard your opinion of your
mother and me. Now it's my turn. You're utterly self-centered, undisciplined, unstable. You make no attempt to
curb your temper or your self-indulgence. Don't worry about
your heredity, that's not to blame. I sired you, God forgive
me! to be an affliction to your mother and a burden to yourself. I'm not proud of you, believe me. Nor am I ashamed
of your origins. What distresses me is that you're not fit to
be our son. I'm glad you're called Brandon. Keep the name,
remembering what is due to the man who protected you

and the brother and sister who'd do credit to better stock. If you ever want to know how to behave, study your brother Geoffrey. You could have no better example. John Brandon has been luckier than I have. But whether I like it or not, I am your father, and your mother's husband. Her reputation is mine. I shall protect it. You won't call her, on any occasion, what you called her just now. If you do, I'll kill you, and I've killed many men before, better, more efficient fighters than you. I've been trained and adapted for violence. I even like it. But do you know where it leads? To corpses and medals and I've had plenty of both in my time. At Meisterhafen, I killed eight men with my bare hands within the hour, and God knows how many more I despatched indirectly. I'm warning you, Michael, son or not, peace or war, I stand no nonsense from such as you, and emotional dictatorship is as unpleasant as any other form of the vice."

"I hate you . . . ," the boy stammered.

"Would you believe it!" I was shocked to hear genuine amusement in Ronan's voice. "I always wanted a son; it was the dream of a lifetime. But you, Mike, are more like a nightmare! Talking of Meisterhafen brings it all back. There was a hell of a long lonely wait, as often happens, and I got to imagining . . . well . . . what a boy of mine could be like. It never occurred to me I'd find someone like you, grown so big and stupid, a slight person of no quality—and you, your mother's son. I've finished with you anyway. You're not what I wanted. I prefer your brother. Get out! And stay out! It's my first and last parental advice."

I can't repeat what I later said to my husband—or what he said to me. Ronan was seldom at a loss for words, and he had leashed tongue and temper, he claimed, for a long hour. Nothing pleased him better than to offload accumulations of self-control, and I gave him every encouragement.

We wore thin. People do. Only the backwash remained.

"This crisis was foist on me without adequate briefing from you. So I dealt with a Grant, using Grant instincts. He didn't like the father which you so kindly provided; very well, try him with another! He was looking for a scrap, forgetting it takes two to play. I've merely given him something to get his teeth into with the postscript that violence breeds its own self-destruction."

He watched me, his eyes devoid of sympathy as I sniffed into my handkerchief. "You've reared a proper mother's boy," he added for good measure, "and a nasty customer. The less he sees of you for a while, the better. It will be interesting to find out what he's really made of, when the issue is less clouded. Not that I'm overeager to come to my conclusions. At this moment, I feel a strong and urgent desire to put anyone who has ever borne the name of Brandon out of my mind for the rest of this evening. And that, my dear wife, goes for you too! If you want a job to keep your mind off your husband-substitute, you can transfer my gear into the dressing room."

"I'm not your servant. Put it there yourself!"

He shrugged and slammed the door behind him.

I was left alone in a state of indecision. Did I want to wait around for the telephone call which undoubtedly would tell me exactly how and where his life had ended? What was left for him to live by, my fine, favourite boy? When the bell did ring, my heart missed at least three beats. But it was only the reception desk reporting Mrs. Anglesey was below, craving admittance. I clicked automatically into deception, recalling wryly that my aunt had this reputation of burying hatchets when everyone else wished to brandish them.

"I was thinking of your drawing room," she cheerfully

announced without preamble. "From all you say, it needs contrast. What have you over the fireplace?"

"A ghesso mirror . . . Chippendale, I think."

"Far too obvious. Now, Mitty, I believe I've found the perfect answer. Saw it in Bond Street today. A ridiculous price of course. You'll have to count it as a wedding present. It's called *Design for Living*."

She fussed with an immense quantity of brown paper and produced an abstract, blending harsh pinks with delicate limes. Two fierce, swirling masses of leaden paint menaced its basic charm and balance. Design for whose life? Mine? But two patches of shadow only! Well, I was deep-shrouded in one of them!

"*Interesting*," I said judiciously. It was Geoffrey's favourite art remark, when words otherwise failed him. I began to smile more naturally—not that she looked.

"I'm coming round to the idea of young Grant," she continued graciously. "I didn't know love and logic could be bedfellows. Amusing to see how it all works out. Ought I to apologize? No! You should have confided in me, if only for practical reasons. As for your husband, I'm relieved to see he's looking much better."

I was able to while away the visit, and I confess my aunt's stiff grey evening silk was so traditional as to be oddly soothing.

Ronan came back at midnight.

"You reek of whisky," I remarked coldly.

"I've been drinking it, that's why. But I'm still in possession of my faculties. One has one's obligations to the young."

"Michael?" I was pathetically eager.

"No, thank God! Geoffrey. I found him downstairs in his best suit, a nervous ambassador presenting credentials to stepfather. I took him out to celebrate my acquisition of that jewel, his Mum. A good thing someone has a sense of humour."

"You told him about Mike?"

"No, I took the obvious opportunity, my loyal love, of enlarging on your undiscovered virtues, and detailing my fouler vices. We talked exhaustively, *and* exhaustingly, of the glories of True Love, which, of course, by interpretation equals Carolyn. After which, I proceeded to my club to imbibe sufficient liquor to take the taste of young worship out of my mouth. The result, you see."

"I've been here all evening. Trying to make up my mind to leave you once and for all."

"But you can't, can you? We're landed with the need to keep a bold front, and not lose face whatever else goes by the board. Geoff, in my opinion, has had just about all he can stand. Then there's that little girl too. As for Mike, he mustn't know you were here this evening, *ever*. And he must be left to work out his salvation. I'm not going to have him tampered with at this stage. It's my job, I'm afraid, a little late, to protect him from you. I didn't enjoy this evening either, and frankly, if it had been the right thing to do, I'd have gladly put my hands in my pockets at the operative time, so I could now be lying in your outraged arms, with a steak over each eye. A charming *mis-en-scène!* Whoever loses gets the sympathy! But it would have solved nothing. Hell, Mari! I married you to get us out of this tangle, not ravel it up into a snarl."

I rubbed my temples despairingly. "I've failed so utterly, I see that now. Yet I only wished to be fair to each of them. How can one pick and choose loves and obligations? Even Johnny depended on me. I was muddled by the weight of it all. I must be very weak and stupid. And if all was to do again, I've the oddest feeling, I'd repeat my mistakes. Johnny didn't ask to be the way he was. As to the children . . .

they were such a delight . . . I was so proud of them. And they were fond of me too in their various ways. I suppose they still are. Mike; I know he sounded silly, but he only wanted to protect me. I suppose I did make him into you, and it was too much for a little boy."

"Hush, my love, don't cry so dreadfully! Don't fret so much. Try and see your old children with new eyes. But you'd be wise to trust me, love, while you get your second wind. Supposing we get to hell out of here . . . go down to Sussex tomorrow? Lord! I've never had to think of so many people in my life before! I can see it might be exhausting. What about bed?"

"Your things are in the dressing room," I pointed out tartly.

"Like hell they are!"

When he laughed outright, it was always appallingly infectious.

"I never did get around to it," I admitted.

"Oh my darling, you're smiling. Let's disagree but don't let's be enemies. We have to make a success of this."

"I thought love conquered all," I retorted.

"Marriage," he said, "is more often a question of endurance."

CHAPTER 24

Ignoring the family, we made guarded small talk all the way to the Grange the next morning.

"Having cricked my back playing James Bond yesterday, I won't volunteer to carry you over the threshold. Besides, I want a word with Pullen," Ronan said as he parked the Bentley.

I walked into the hall reluctantly, to be halted by a great floral extravagance centered on the gate-leg table. And so beautifully arranged! There was a trickery, of displaying each bloom to full advantage which was reminiscent.

"Hello Mum!"

Renata was standing in the library doorway. I realized at once she was the one person in the world I really wanted to see. I was tired of menfolk.

"You!" I hugged her. "Ren, where did you spring from? And like magic!"

"You're not angry with me? Oh, that's a relief! 'Cos it wasn't my fault. I was more or less kidnapped by stepfather and a smashing chauffeur with a Tony Curtis haircut. Aunt was out. You were shopping, and here I am! He wouldn't take no for an answer."

"Darling, it's marvellous. Makes all the difference."

"Gosh! I hope you mean that. I said I had to make myself scarce, and was told that pretty stepdaughters were scarce enough already, and it was my duty to come ahead and see everything was just so. Actually it's so spit-and-polishy, I could only think of flowers. Aren't they fabulous! I was driven in a Rolls too. First time ever. And you know Pullen, Mum? He was born in Pargiton. In one of those cottages by the church, and the grocer's redhead is his cousin."

She paused for breath. Even Ren does sometimes.

"Lay off Pullen," I said, "or Annette will have your eyes out."

"That's just what Ronan said. He's fun, isn't he? I dig stepfathers."

"Extraordinary thing to do!" The gentleman in question now came indoors. I was glad to see him looking sheepish. "Vaguely archaeological. Possibly macabre."

"She's done the flowers," I said repressively.

"Good God! So she has! McGregor's prize chrysanthemums too. I'll never live this down."

"Do you mean old Capability Brown with the whiskers? But he's the *most!* He said it was a grrrand occasion for the Grrrange, and he liked fine to see a bonnie, sonsy lassie wi' a bunch o' flowers tae her, or something equally Caledonian. He waxed most poetic."

From that moment, no one seriously questioned who ran the Grange or its gardens. Renata was transported.

"Did you ever see such a place, Mum?" She followed to heel wherever we went. "To think I'm going to live here!"

I noted with astonishment that right from the first Renata was more comfortable with Ronan than with me or the boys. She connected him, I think, with massive security, and I had to admit she must have been lonely and troubled for longer than I knew. But now relief simmered and boiled over. She was ecstatic.

"Don't blame me," I said to her new guardian when at last we were alone. "For some reason, you asked her. Now you've got her."

"Wasn't I right? I'm sorry, love. It wasn't intentional deception. I felt sure I should have a private word with her. Not much fun to lose school and home both together. A little conspiracy of some sort seemed indicated. As soon as we began talking, I knew half-measures were mean somehow. And when I hit on this—you should have seen her face!"

"It was good of you," I said. So it was, but I wasn't used to having family decisions taken out of my hands, however successful the outcome. As it happened, it was an excellent idea. The child's gaiety and enthusiasm made it easier for us to settle down behind her smoke screen. So the Grange

blossomed subtly into life and disorder, and if Ronan regretted more meticulous days, he was patient.

We had very little privacy. For years, she had been drifting in and out of my bedroom, either to drench herself with
my scent or borrow my luxuries. Nor did she see reason to
change the Brandon order of Sunday morning.

"You don't mind, do you?" she would inquire disarmingly,
sitting firmly on our feet and watching us drink morning
tea. "I've been up for hours and everybody's busy except
you."

"Ren, do sit on a chair," I protested weakly.

"Sorry! But somehow double beds are so comfortable!
Aunt Peg and Uncle Arthur go in for twin ones. I think
that's a mistake. I wonder if they're happy—really, I mean.
I've been thinking a lot about marriage and sex lately. I
realize you're newly-weds, and I suppose people are just as
bad at any age. But do you think Aung Peg and Uncle Arthur were ever demonstrative? Even when they were young?
Now look at Ronan. He even calls me *love* by accident,
which is very nice. I like it. Still, I suppose, it's different altogether. Ronan's been a sort of bachelor for ages, and
they're more handy with women. I expect it's because they
have dozens of mistresses and get in practice."

Ronan nearly spilt his tea.

"You flatter me, *love*," he emphasized. "My constitution
for mistresses was poor. Not dozens please—the thought of
them before breakfast distresses me. Couldn't we postpone
my private life, and your unspeakable Uncle Arthur's, till
some more appropriate hour?"

The trouble was she took him at his word.

"I've been thinking," she later settled down on the hearthrug, a kitten in her lap, to make a very pretty picture. "I'm
hopeless at playing gooseberry. Not through lack of advice,
I've had that. But it's difficult. I like being with you. It's

heaven to *belong*. But you will boot me out, Ronan, won't you, if I'm a pest? The boys do."

"You're no great trouble, Ren." He smiled.

We had settled down into a sort of tentative routine when Geoffrey asked himself down for the weekend. It was his first visit and he seemed an outsider. Ren, Ronan, and I exchanged a family glance, wondering if he were ill or just miserable. I noticed my daughter was already more sensitive to other people, though her determined efforts to cheer up her brother were a little overpowering. By Saturday night, he looked dead on his feet, and I thought it as well that she was booked for a party at the Garlands.

"Freddie Logan will bring me home. I don't know when."

"I've told Pullen to fetch you at eleven-thirty, when Connie Garland says the party will be over."

"It's not fair. I'm not a kid."

"Seventeen, Renata, and in my care. We'll argue it out tomorrow, for if we start now, you'll be late."

"Gosh! So I will."

She ran off. Geoffrey was grinning.

"Stone the crows!" he said inelegantly. "Who'd have thought it? You were cut out for step-paternity, Ronan. Not a tear, not a pout. Just dubious feminine submission."

"Actually I quite enjoy my new hobby," Ronan said. "Can I give you any parental advice, Geoff?"

"Well, I am a bit fussed."

"You look worn-out, G.," I put in anxiously. "Are you overworking?"

"You could say I was," he replied. "I've an evening job too."

"I wish you wouldn't. It's bad for you and for your career."

"I can manage for myself, of course, but there's Carolyn. I can't take her on a shoestring."

"Do her good," Ronan said unsympathetically.

"Do you know until she started hanging round my flat, she couldn't scramble eggs. Now I make her do all the cooking while she's there. But I tell her, it's one thing to play houses, and quite another to keep them."

"What's this in aid of, G.? Marriage?" I asked.

"I don't know. I meant to do it properly, but I'm beginning to feel she'd be better with me, even as I am, than with that ghastly mother of hers. Do you know, she has some beastly old man in tow, an Armenian or something. Fabulously rich, and he's crazy about my pretty. I can't bear to think of her even talking to him, and there she is, at the same house for the weekend, and Mrs. L.M. working like a beaver."

"What does Carolyn think about all this?"

"Now she's twenty-one, she's keen on marrying and hoping for the best."

"Why not? I'd expect her to be cleverer at contrivance than you are, Geoff. And hang it all! You don't have to starve and she knows it. Also she knows, for she's cute that way, that the situation is quite different since I came into the picture, and that I'm likely to consider your mother's children as my own."

The boy looked awkward and hung his head to draw patterns on the chair arm with his forefinger.

"I know now how Mum felt in the old days. You can be proud on your own behalf, but not when people you are fond of are involved. I know your loan to Mike was phony, but I was wondering, if it were done in a really businesslike manner, whether you could tide me over, just till I qualify. I'd pay back just as soon as I could. I had thought of Aunt Anglesey, but I'd rather it was you, sir."

"*Sir?* Since when, Geoff? You can have what you damned like, you know that. My only worry is that you won't ask for

216

enough. You won't be able to afford interest, and we'll secure it on your inheritance, shall we? I'm bound to leave you something out of pure decency! I take it as a great compliment that you should come to me. You're not my son, Geoff, but your generosity, throughout a very difficult phase, makes me wish you were. I myself have only one condition —that you give up this sideline work, and save your energies for architecture."

"I'm most grateful. But I will repay you."

"You can do that best by making a success of your marriage, which is usually a matter of pure resolution, I'm afraid. It would give us both great pleasure if you could find what we've missed—and the sooner the better. Life's short."

At first I was relieved when Ren went off to visit a schoolfriend in Wales, but the pleasure we anticipated at having the house to ourselves was not realized. In the sudden quiet, there was new stimulus to active thought on the one subject we never discussed, and the one important person always missing from the family circle.

From the moment he had staggered out of the hotel suite, I had had no word of Michael. He faded into thin air and apparently communicated with no one. At first, I accepted this as inevitable, but now some considerable time had elapsed and I began to grow seriously worried. There were so many horrors one could imagine, all with good reason.

Mostly I kept them to myself. When I did not I was told Mike was so like Gavin the same medicine could be prescribed for both. I was told I didn't understand my own son; that he was a Grant and quite beyond my simple comprehension.

I was, of course, far too involved with Mike, feeling for him and thinking about him; he was on my mind night and day. Nor was I at all ready to hand over my policies and responsibilities to anyone, least of all to Ronan.

One evening I finally forced out what I wanted. Furious, Mike might have gone anywhere.

"All right," said Ronan wearily. "Mike's in London. He never left town, and is selling cars, quite successfully, I believe, and learning, I profoundly hope, manners and discipline in the process. Possibly enough time has elapsed. . . . You may have his address tomorrow."

Ronan even ran me into London and settled me in a hotel. He pecked my cheek and wished me luck. . . . Mike wasn't available till evening. At last I caught my tube-train and emerged into grim, littered streets, relieved when Mike's address brought me to a row of bigger houses. His landlady was clean and respectable. I climbed the stairs slowly.

The door was ajar and relief flooded me to see him standing at the window. Thank God, I thought suddenly, that he knows who he is! "Michael," I said quietly. "I am so sorry."

"Mother! The last person I expected. Come in. Not much of a place, but the idea is to pay back Aunt Trix as soon as I can."

"Ronan told me what happened at that hotel, and that he'd known where you were ever since."

"I daresay he thought, and fair enough, I'd be better on my own. I did have rather a hefty shock. Give me some credit for keeping out of the way until I'd come to terms. Did he tell you we came to blows?"

"It was a disgraceful business!"

"That's true. I've lived with it, and wondered if I could ever hold up my head again. Oh, I didn't enjoy facing up to the bar sinister, and still less that I'd behaved like my kind. Yet, even so, there was a rush of relief as if an enormous burden had been lifted. I wasn't John Brandon's son after all. When I'd absorbed that with gratitude it was like living in a new world. All my life I've been stuck in the wrong groove, and vaguely aware of it. I was different. You treated me differently. Now I know where I am. It's better. Why should you apologize? Grant bloody well didn't. So it was up to me to make the first approach. The letter should be at Stoke Hempstead by now."

"So you did make overtures? I'm glad. But there was nothing for me this morning."

"I wrote to my Father, actually. It's not your business. He'd want to think it over. He accepts that I'm his son; I suppose he'd prefer me installed in a decent profession instead of flogging cars all my life. I'm only suggesting a modified version of the old arrangement. I'm even prepared to pay him back."

"Oh, Michael! I've heard everything now."

"What do you expect? That I ask him what it feels like to father a cheap bully? You know who he *is*, don't you? He *was* the Meisterhafen raid. You never told me. And all the time I was R. J. Grant's son!"

"Then why quarrel with him, even as a stepfather?"

"Do you think I realized? Grant's a commonish name. It didn't click till too late. I don't suppose he'll ever speak to me again. But I've one ambition and my Father can afford to pay for it. At least I'll make the grade on my own, and he knows it."

"Ronan will give you the money, I don't doubt."

"He's not a bad sort of a chap, surely?"

"No." I smiled. "Not really."

I said goodbye gratefully. Children! If only they were less irritatingly *young!*

A taxi took me home, home to the trustworthy and the mature, home to a sense of proportion and humour. Home to Ronan.

"My love, you look dead! Sit yourself down by the fire and tell me about it."

"Shall I burst into tears or laugh my head off?"

"You had to get it over."

"I know. But it was so different from anything I expected. And that he should have asked you for money!"

"He's a Scot, darling, stiff-necked and stiff-kneed. It's no accident we Presbyterians eschew the hassock. And what else could he do? It's the obvious approach. He's just like Gavin. It makes me laugh. Offload on me while you can, for you'll have more to bear before that boy straightens out finally."

"But will he, Ronan?"

"Ach, yes. He's doing fine. Now we have to get him back to his favorite grindstone as soon as we can."

"He's fallen for your medals."

"I thought he might. Pretty things if you don't have to win them. I suppose he's looking for a hero to take the taste of your John out of his mouth. Let's hope it does the trick."

"He's fonder of you than me, Ronan. Could I be jealous?"

"Why? Let's share out for a change. Give Mike the chance to spread his affections rather wider."

"I don't want to pull against you, darling."

"Then pull toward me now. Make up for lost time."

I did, and very peaceful it was.

"What are you thinking of, love?" he asked after a long silence.

"Not a great deal," I replied lazily. "I was feeling this might be a very happy ending, and it reminded me of the beginning. Friend Dante! His dark wood, the trees overgrowing, and no light anywhere."

"But you've never seen it from the outside, your *selva oscura*. Ach, love, but it's a bonnie wood, with fine trees in

220

it, and you walking among them, so a man could ache to be there with you."

"It's like a book. Not that anybody would believe a word of it. When you come to consider, it's the oddest sort of love story."

"It's not a love story, it's a story about love," Ronan said.

And so it is!